From The Women's Press Ltd
124 Shoreditch High Street, London E1

Janet Frame

Janet Frame was born in Dunedin, New Zealand, in 1924. Her works include ten novels, among them *A State of Siege, Scented Gardens for the Blind* (The Women's Press 1982) *Living in the Maniototo* (The Women's Press 1981) and *Faces in the Water* (The Women's Press 1980); also four collections of stories and sketches, including *You Are Now Entering The Human Heart* (The Women's Press, 1984), a volume of poetry and a children's book, *Mona Minim and the Smell of the Sun. To The Is-land*, the first volume of her autobiography, was published by The Women's Press in 1983, and won the James Wattie Book of the Year award. The second volume, *An Angel At My Table*, was published by The Women's Press in 1984. Janet Frame was awarded the CBE in the 1983 Queen's Birthday Honours List. She has been a Burns Scholar, won the New Zealand Scholarship in Letters and the Hubert Church award for prose, was awarded an honorary doctorate in Literature by the University of Otago, and in 1980 won the Fiction Prize, New Zealand Book Awards for *Living in the Maniototo*.

Janet Frame
Owls Do Cry

The Women's Press

Published in Great Britain by
The Women's Press Limited 1985
A member of the Namara Group
124 Shoreditch High Street, London E1 6JE

First published by WH Allen and Co. Ltd
Pegasus Press Ltd 1961

British Library Cataloguing in Publication Data

Frame, Janet
Owls do cry.
I. Title
823(F)   PR9639.3.F7

ISBN 0-7043-3958-7

Printed and bound in Great Britain
by Nene Litho and Woolnough Bookbinding
both of Wellingborough, Northants

Where the bee sucks, there suck I;
In a cowslip's bell I lie;
There I couch when owls do cry;
On the bat's back I do fly,
After summer, merrily.

THE TEMPEST

Part One
Talk of Treasure

1

        The day is early with birds beginning and the wren in a cloud piping like the child in the poem, drop thy pipe, thy happy pipe. And the place grows bean flower, pea-green lush of grass, swarm of insects dizzily hitting the high spots; dunny rosette creeping covering shawl cream in a knitted cosy of roses; ah the tipsy wee small hours of insects that jive upon the crippled grass blades and the face of the first flower alive; and I planted carrot seed that never came up, for the wind breathed a blow-away spell; the wind is warm, was warm, and the days above burst unheeded, explode their atoms of snow-black beanflower and white rose, mock the last intuitive who-dunnit, who-dunnit of the summer thrush; and it said to plant the carrot seeds lightly under a cotton-thin blanket of earth, yet they sank too deep or dried up, and the blackfly took hold among the beans that flowered later in midnight velvet, and I thought I might have known, which is the thought before the stealth of fate; lush of summer, yes, but what use the green river, the gold place, if time and death pinned human in the pocket of my land not rest from taking underground the green all-willowed and white rose and bean flower and morning-mist picnic of song in pepper-pot breast of thrush?
And now, voluminous, dyspeptic Santa Claus, there is a mound of snow at the door of Christmas that no midsummer day or human sun will dispel, and it is that way, and seems that way, to fit in; and now do we buy a Christmas card and write or sign the obituary of string with sticky tape; wrap our life in cellophane with a handkerchief and card; buy a caterpillar that is wound up and crawls with rippling back across our day and night.
Sings Daphne from the dead room.

2

Their grandmother was a negress who had long ago been a slave with her long black dress and fuzzy hair and oily skin, in the Southern States of America. She sang often of her home,

—Carry me back to ole Virginny,
    there's where the cotton an' the corn an' taters grow,
    there's where the birds warble sweet in the spring-time,
    there's where my old darkie's heart am long to go.

And now that she is dead she will have returned to Virginny and be walking through the cotton fields, with the sun shining on her frizzy hair that is like a ball of black cotton to be danced on or thistledown that birds take for living in if their world be black.

No, you must eat your cabbage, for colanders hang on the wall that cabbage may be pressed through them, that the green water may run out; though if you have diabetes you must drink the green water or you may, like your grandmother, lose two legs, and have new wooden ones made, that you keep behind the door, in the dark, and that have no knees to bend, no toes to wiggle.

Colander?

Colander?

Calendar?

Calendars hang upon the wall and have bills pinned to them from the grocer and milkman and butcher; and somehow they contrive in hanging there to collect all the days and months of the year, numbering them, like convicts, in case they escape.

Which they do, always.

—Time flies, said Mrs Withers. And it is calendar, not colander, you silly children. Francie, Toby, Daphne, Chicks, drink up your cabbage water or you shall lose two legs, like your grandmother.

3

I don't wanner go to school, Toby said. I wanner go to the rubbish dump an' find things.

Francie, Toby, Daphne, not always Chicks because she was too small and dawdled, found their treasure at the rubbish dump, amongst the paper and steel and iron and rust and old boots and everything that the people of the town had cast out as of no use and not worth anything any more. The place was like a shell with gold tickle of toi-toi around its edges and grass and weeds growing in green fur over the mounds of rubbish; and from where the children sat, snuggled in the hollow of refuse, warmed sometimes by the trickling streams of fires that the council men had lit in order to hasten the death of their material cast-offs, they could see the sky passing in blue or grey ripples, and hear in the wind, the heavy fir tree that leaned over the hollow, rocking, and talking to itself saying firr-firr-firr, its own name, loosening its needles of rust that slid into the yellow and green burning shell to prick tiny stitches across the living and lived-in wound where the children found, first and happiest, fairy tales.

And a small green eaten book by Ernest Dowson who said, in confidence, to Cynara,

—Last night ah yesternight betwixt her lips and mine.

Which was love, and suitable only for Francie who had *come*, that was the word their mother used when she whispered about it in the bathroom, and not for Daphne who didn't know what it felt like or how she could wear them without they showed and people said, Look.

—You will drop blood when you walk, Francie said.

And not knowing how to answer her, Daphne said

—Rapunsel, Rapunsel, let down your hair;

quoting from the prince who climbed the gold silk rope to the top of the tower, it was all in the fairy tales they found at the rubbish dump. The book smelt, and it too had been eaten by worms which still lived in its yellow pages, and it was dusted over with ashes, and it had been thrown away because it did not any more speak the right language, and the people could not read it because they could not find the way to its world. It had curly writing on the cover, saying, The Brothers Grimm. It spoke of Cinderella and her ugly sisters with their cut-off heel and toe and the blood flowing black, the snow colour of every bean flower.

—But I don't wanner go to school, Toby said. I wanner go to the rubbish dump an' find another book.

The lady doctor was coming to school that day. She wore

a grey costume and because she was the school nurse and fierce, they had her mixed in their mind with the grey nurse shark that is deadly, creeping behind you when you swim, to swallow you in one gulp; though not found in these waters, only, I believe, near Sydney.

Every time she came the nurse took the dirty children to look at them and whisper at them through a roll of cardboard. Thirty-two, fifty-five, sixty-one, she would whisper; and the children, if they were the dirty ones and being examined, would have to echo, Thirty-two, fifty-five, sixty-one; and if they echoed correctly it meant they could hear and would not have their ears poked at and operated on. And the lady doctor would then take a stick like an ice-cream spoon and very very gently part the strands of the pupil's hair, to look through it and find if it were inhabited. She would look at their clothes, too, and see how often they had been washed, and if they were hand-me-downs or new. And she would hold a square of cardboard in front of the dirty children and point to the letters printed on it, and expect to be told the alphabet, muddled up, and them to see small print, even smaller than the middle column of a page of the Bible where it says See Tim. Rom. Deut., and other mysterious words.

Toby did not like this. He feared it all. He had seen on a page of the doctor's book that his mother kept on top of the wardrobe, a picture of the animals with many legs that walk through people's hair; and the red spots that come on people's faces, and the way legs turn crooked. Toby was a sick boy, himself, who took medicine, a teaspoon in water after each meal until his mother found out what the writing on the prescription meant. And then,

—Bromide, she said. Drugs.

So whenever the bottle of medicine came, in twos or repeats, Toby's mother said

—No child of mine, no child of mine will drink this filth; and she broke the seal and popped off the cork and poured away the thick mulatto fluid.

Toby did not get better. He went to school and sat in the back row and put his head on one side, trying to know what was written on the blackboard and what the master, Andy Reid, was saying in the history lesson.

There had been Maori Wars and the white people had taken a block of land—how big is a block of land, Toby wondered. They built houses with blocks and walked in the morning around the block, touching every second fence and plucking every third marigold. But this block of land in history, they say it held a forest of kauri that only a storm could walk round in a minute and pull out by the hair, every second and third tree.

—The government was good then, Andy would say.

And sometimes he said—The government was bad.

And he talked of peace and war that never seemed to happen at the same time in history. There were, say, six years of peace when Maoris and white people spent every day and night of the years smiling at each other and rubbing noses and exchanging greenstone and kumaras and kauri and marrying and going for picnics and boiling the billy and drinking tea and eating fish and laughing and no one was ever angry.

Until the six years finished. On New Year's Eve, perhaps, with the white and brown people standing outside the New Year, the same way people stand outside theatres and cricket grounds waiting for the films or the shield match to begin; and the mothers warning their children, Remember you must not laugh or play or swap anything. We are killing for six years. It is War.

Toby could not imagine years of war, but Andy Reid told everyone and Andy Reid knew. He said also that there had been a Hundred Years' War when some people's faces must have been born angry and died angry without any smiling in between.

But history was hard to understand with its kings good and bad and their wigs and their white fitting pants for dancing a minuet; and then the two princes sitting in the dreadful tower and listening to the water dripping from an underground cavern on to their faces and down their necks and on their heads poked like flowers from their pretty petal ruffs. Toby felt sorry for them but he could not understand history and wanting to get more land and gold; nor, sometimes, could he understand what the master said, or read the words on the blackboard. And that is why he wanted not to go to school when the lady doctor came.

He was often sick and had to stay away from school. When he was sick his hand shook as if it felt cold and then a dark cloak would be thrown over his head by Jesus or God, and he would struggle inside the cloak, pushing at the velvet folds, waving his arms and legs in the air till the sun took pity, descending in a dazzling crane of light to haul, but, alas, preserve, where in all the sky, Toby wondered, this cloak of stifling recurring dream. And he would open his eyes and see his mother beside him, her big tummy and the map of wet and flour on her sack apron.

He would cry then.

The velvet cloak came over and over again so that whenever Toby moved his hand or arm too quickly, his mother would rush to his side and ask,

—Are you all right, Toby?

Or at school Andy Reid would say,

—You can go and lie down, Toby Withers, and you may be able to stop it.

—It?

Did Andy Reid understand what happened, and how the cloak came with its forest of a million folds? Did he know why some people are given a private and lonely night, with a room of its own but no window that the stars, called by the tattered woman at the show *Zodiac*, may look through?

So Toby did not go to school that day when the lady doctor came. He said goodbye to his mother and father and said,

—Yes, I've got a hanky and I'll tell them if *it* comes on; and he ran on ahead of Daphne. Daphne was glad, for it made her afraid to be close to him in case it happened and she was alone watching him, and he would die or choke out of the terrible mulberry colour of his face and his hands twitching and his eyes rolled back, and white, like the eye, closed, of a dead fowl that Daphne had seen by the fowl house. And yet, standing there on the wet side of the street, with Toby gone ahead, and the African Thorn hedge, hung with berries like penny oranges, leaning over to jag her legs if she walked too close, she felt alone, and wanted to catch up; so she caught up and went with Toby to the rubbish dump to find things. They found a bicycle wheel and a motor tyre. Inside the motor tyre was a stack of ledgers full of neat writing and figures written carefully in a beautiful blue ink; and each page seemed, to the children, like something out of a museum, to be kept under a glass case, like the handwriting of a pioneer or governor.

Daphne gathered the books and put them in her lap, stroking them because they were valuable.

—These are treasures, she said. Better than silver paper, this lovely writing.

—They're not, said Toby. They're just sums, grown-up sums.

—But they're made like treasures. Why do they throw them away? And when you're grown up you work at treasure, so it must be.

—No. It's out of banks, said Toby. Where they wear striped suits and get red in the face when it's hot.

And he tore some pages out of the books, though Daphne tried to hold on to them, and he made paper aeroplanes and wet on one to see if it changed to invisible.

And then they talked about the fairy tales that nobody had wanted and had put in the ashes to be burned. There was a little man, truly, the size of a thumb. He used to drive a horse by sitting in the horse's ear and whispering Whoa or Gee-up. And there was a king who lived in a mountain of glass and could see his face in seventy different mirrors in one look. And a table that rose up through the earth the way the organ, they say, in the big theatres, rises through the floor and music plays before the people are settled and *God Save the Queen* begins.

And to make the table vanish the little girl in the story had to say only,

—Bleat goat bleat
  Depart table neat.

—But, talking of tables, I'm hungry, Daphne said to Toby. What've we got?

They had nothing. Dinner time must be close, they thought, so they took one page of the blue writing of sums, in case it was really treasure for a glass case, and they walked home, passing the fruit shop on the way.

Daphne went into the shop that seemed always wet and being washed and the cabbages turning yellow and the fruit specked; and before the shopkeeper came (she was a Chinese woman with different funerals and weddings and churches from Toby and Daphne) Daphne sneaked an apple under her arm and crept out, so that she and Toby had half an apple each, dividing it fairly because it really belonged to Daphne, Toby having the green sour part with thick skin, and Daphne the rosy-cheeked side; though to emphasize the fairness of their venture and the importance of not telling, she agreed to let him walk on the sunny side of the street and be warm while she continued in the shade.

And in the afternoon they both went to school. The lady doctor had been. She had collected people and ticked off their names on white cards, with red ink, and given Norris Stevens a note to take home to his mother, about his tonsils. He was to have his tonsils out, he said, and everyone felt envious.

—Why were you not at school this morning, Miss Drout said to Daphne.

—I was sick, Daphne said.

And

—It came, was Toby's answer to Andy Reid. And Toby was told to lie on the sick bed and they gave him a drink of milk at playtime, through a straw.

4

Their town, called Waimaru, was small as the world and halfway between the South Pole and the equator, that is, forty-five degrees exactly. There was a stone monument just north of the town, to mark the spot, in gold lettering.

—Traveller, the writing said, Stop here. You are now standing halfway between the South Pole and the equator.

What did it feel like to be standing at forty-five degrees? It felt no different.

Waimaru was a respectable town with the population increasing so quickly that the Mayor kept being forced to call special meetings of the borough council, which were reported in the local newspaper, the rag, it was called. To decide if the reserves where grew native trees and shrubs should be offered for sale as housing sections, and the shrubs, and also the children who played near them after school, be rooted out and planted somewhere else; but the Mayor's suggestion was defeated and letters to the paper followed, threats of resignation, a special meeting of the afraid beautifying society who had given many shrubs; a defiant meeting of the Build Your Own Home Club; after which, calm fell like a sweet mantle, and the shrubs and children (including the Withers family) remained happily planted on the hills surrounding the town.

And the young Councillors shook their heads, saying,

—This is not progress. The northern towns go ahead, becoming bigger and bigger, while we stagnate here, in the south.

They were afraid.

—We shall be left behind, they said.

Left behind from going where?

Among the letters to the paper were some by Mrs Withers who called herself Tui, the native bird, to show she wanted the native bush left on the hills. And sometimes she called herself, if she were writing about bush, Miro, the little red berry. She showed her children the letters, and though they could not understand them, they knew their mother must be Someone, so they could say it in school, with the others who said,

—My father owns a car.

—My uncle can chop down trees faster than anyone.

—My mother writes letters to the paper.

—Yes, Mrs Withers would say, as she licked the envelope for closing,

—I'll blow them up.

And Bob, her husband, would make a rude remark to her.

—Yes, I'll blow them up. I'll put my foot down. We women can't be trodden on.

Sometimes, instead of signing herself Tui, she became Mother of Four; and instead of Miro, the little red berry, she changed to Disgusted, or, merely and universally, A Mother.

—I see Mother of Three has answered me, she would say. I'll settle her.

Oh, as if gentle Amy Withers could settle anyone!

And then her husband, going to a lodge meeting, would call from the bedroom,

—Where's my best tartan tie? I haven't all the time in the world.

And Amy Withers would pick over shirts and socks till she was hit by a cascade of tartan tie.

—Here's your tie, Bob.

She was afraid of her husband. She said Sh-sh to the children when Bob came home from work or parliament was on the air.

—Honorable gentlemen, Bob would say.

Honorable gentlemen.

He was Labour.

But, about the town. You should read a booklet that you may buy for five shillings and sixpence, reduced at sale time to five shillings, increased at Christmas to six shillings. This booklet will tell you the important things about the town and show you photographs—the town clock saying ten to three (the correct position of the hands for driving, says the local traffic inspector); the begonia house at the Gardens, and a perplexed-looking little man who must be the curator, holding a begonia plant in flower; the roses in the rose arch and the ferns in the fernery; also a photograph of the Freezing Works, the outside with its own garden and fancy flower-beds, and the inside with rows of pegged pigs with their tiny trotters thrust out stiff; of the Woollen Mills, the chocolate factory, the butter factory, the flour mill—all meaning prosperity and wealth and a fat filled land; and lastly a photograph of the foreshore with its long sweep of furious and hungry water, the roll-down sea the children call it, where you cannot bathe without fear of the undertow, and you bathe carefully, as you live, between the flags; and beware of the tentacles of sea-weed and the rush of pebbles being sucked back and back into the sea's mouth each time it draws breath. Certainly, inside the breakwater is a little shovel-scoop of bay, Friendly Bay, where you paddle and sail shells and eat ice cream bought from Peg Winter, the mountainous woman who moves like faith from town to town, leaving behind her a trail of sweet and ice-cream shops, almost as if they dropped from her pocket, like crumbs or seeds springing into red and white painted shape, with cream-coloured tables and chairs inside, and other high swivel-chairs as the dizzying accompaniment to a caramel or strawberry milk shake.

And glass cases packed with chocolate, dark or milk, fruity or plain.

Everything in a glass case is valuable.

5

Sings Daphne from the dead room.
Sometimes in this world I have thought the night will never finish and the real city come no nearer and I think I will stand for a breath under the huge blue-gum trees that I have in my mind. My eyes are used to the dark and as I see the tall trees

with their bark half-stripped and the whitish flesh of trunk revealed underneath, I think of my father saying to me or Toby or Francie or Chicks,

—I'll flay the skin off your hide, I will.

And I know that a wild night wind has spoken those same words to the gum trees. I'll flay the skin off your hide.

And there is the skin hanging in strips. I smell the blue-grey gum-nuts, five ounces of them, flavoured and nobbly under my feet, and I take off my shoes and the gum-nuts dig in my feet and I walk to the foreshore of Waimaru where the sea will creep into the sleep of people and flow round and round in their head, eating out caverns where it echoes and surges till the people become eroded with the green moth and all cry inside themselves, Help, Help.

And then even the sun travels from dark to dark and I am not the sun.

Yes, even the sun.

And why will it rain so much after the night?

Rain.

Up north in the winter-time or midsummer the rain drips in sheets of silver paper, my mother said, who lived there a long time ago, where there are wasps in swarms and a blossom week and palm trees, imported; where the daffodils are earlier than here, with wider and frillier trumpets, and the flowers more bright, painted, growing in the superlatives of memory; and the sea, why the sea more blue and warm and churned in the summer-time with sharks whose presence is reported in the newspapers,

Seen on the green lawn.

And the footpath in the northern city?

It melts under your feet.

And the rain falls in silver paper.

And a kingfisher, colour-fast, will sit on a telegraph wire and be stroked and sing with the silver dazzle.

Oh Francie, Francie was Joan of Arc in the play, wearing a helmet and breastplate of silver cardboard. She was burned, was burned at the stake.

6

It was an afternoon in a hall filled with people, girls in their white spun silk, each holding shilling bags of coconut ice, pink and white, from the home-made sweet stall; mothers who smelled like a closed room of talcum powder and stored fur; with their parcels from the handwork sale, tablerunners and tea-showers in lazy-daisy and chain and shadow stitch.

It was the last day of the term and Francie's last day at school though she was only twelve, thirteen after Christmas. She could count up to thirty in French. She could make puff pastry, dabbing the butter carefully before each fold. She could cook sago, lemon or pink with cochineal, that swelled in cooking from dirty little grains, same, same, dusty and bagged in paper, to lemon or pink pearls. She knew that a drop of iodine on a slice of banana will blacken the fruit, and prove starch; that water is H_2O; that a man called Shakespeare, in a wood near Athens, contrived a moonlit dream.

But in all her knowing, she had not learned of the time of living, the unseen always, when people are like the marbles in the fun alley at the show; and a gaudy circumstance will squeeze payment from their cringing and poverty-stricken fate, to give him the privilege of rolling them into the bright or dark box, till they drop into one of the little painted holes, their niche, it is called, and there roll their lives round and round in a frustrating circle.

And Francie was taken, on the afternoon of the play, like one of the marbles, though still in her silver helmet and breast-plate and waiting to be burned; and rolled to a new place beyond Frère Jacques and participles and science and bunsen burners and Shakespeare, there I couch when owls do cry,
when owls do cry when owls do cry,

To a new place of bright or dark, of home again, and Mum and Dad and Toby and Chicks; an all-day Mum and Dad, as if she were small again, not quite five, with no school, no school ever, and her world, like her tooth, under her pillow with a promise of sixpence and no school ever any more. No black stockings to buy and get on tick with panama hat and blouse and black shoes, with the salesman spearing the account sheets in a terrible, endless ritual, licking the end of the pencil that is chained by a worn gold chain to the counter, carefully writing the prices, totting the account in larger than ordinary figures so as to see and make quite sure, for the Withers are not going to pay yet. It is all on appro. With the deliberation of power then, the salesman plunges the sheet of paper through the metal spear that stands rooted in a small square of wood;

then he moves the wood carefully aside, with the paper speared and torn but spouting no visible blood, and the total unharmed and large, and Francie (or Daphne or Toby or Chicks) staring sideways, afraid, at the committed debt. The Withers are under sentence. It is likely they will be put in prison. And the salesman smooths the sheet of account slips with the power of judgment and fate in the pressure of his hand.

—Will it be all right, the children ask, till the end of the month?

—Certainly, till the end of the month.

But rooted in his mind is the shining awl, the spear to pierce sheaves of accounts and secure them till their day of judgment, to the Last Trump, when the dead spring up like tall boards out of their grave.

But how shall there be room for the dead? They shall be packed tight and thin like malt biscuits or like the pink ones with icing in between that the Withers could never afford; except for Aunty Nettie passing through on the train.

So for Francie now, no black stockings to find and darn or uniform to sponge or panama hat to be cleaned with whiting and water and the time saying, Will you walk a little faster? And the marks not coming off, and Francie crying because Miss Legget inspected the hats and pointed to the ones not clean and floppy and said,

—A disgrace. Now quick march, girls, toes meet the floor first, quick march, but not Francie Withers.

Francie Withers is dirty. Francie Withers is poor. The Withers haven't a week-end bach nor do they live on the South Hill nor have they got a vacuum cleaner nor do they learn dancing or the piano nor have birthday parties nor their photos taken at the Dainty Studio to be put in the window on a Friday.

Francie Withers has a brother who's a shingle short. She couldn't bring the fuji silk for sewing, she had to bring ordinary boiling silk that you shoot peas through, because she's poor. You never see her mother dressed up. They haven't any clothes and Francie hasn't any shoes for changing to at drill time, and her pants are not *real* black Italian cloth.

She hasn't a school blazer with a monogram.

But Francie Withers is Joan of Arc, and she sang at the garden party—

Where the bee sucks there suck I
In a cowslip's bell I lie,
There I couch when owls do cry.
When owls do cry, when owls do cry.

But not any more there I couch when owls do cry. There are owls in the macrocarpa and cabbage trees and they cry quee-will, quee-will, and sometimes at night because of the trees you think it is raining for ever and there will be no more sun, only quee-will and dark.

But the day, for Francie, left school, will be forever, with them all having breakfast and their father going to work, smelling of tobacco and shaving soap and the powder he sprinkles on his feet to stop them from becoming athletic.

—What shift, Bob?

—Late shift, Amy. Home at ten.

But very often he did not call her Amy, only Mother, or Mum, as if she really were his mother.

And she would call him Father, or Dad, as if in marrying him she had found another father.

Besides Francie's grandad.

And besides God.

—Yes, late shift, Amy. Home at ten.

—Oh Dad, you'll never get your sleep in.

—If I'm off tomorrow I'll fix the waste pipe.

—It needs fixing.

—Of course it needs fixing. Haven't I told you time and again not to put grease and stuff down it?

—I've been emptying the dishwater outside, on the roses, to keep the blight away.

—You didn't last night.

—I forgot, Dad.

—Good Lord, is that the time? Make sure you keep those kids away from that rubbish dump, they're the talk of the town, them going and playing in all that rubbish, strikes me they can't tell what's rubbish from what isn't rubbish.

—Yes, Dad.

He almost kisses his wife then, and is gone, wheeling his bike around the corner, and Amy stands looking after him. She wipes her hands on her wet apron, it is always wet, a wide patch of wet where she leans over the sink to wash the dishes.

She thinks for one moment, because she is romantic, of herself and Bob and the time he courted her and sang to her, what was the song—

> Come for a trip in my airship
> come for a trip midst the stars,
> come for a spin around Venus
> come for a trip around Mars;
> no one to watch while we're kissing,
> no one to see while we spoon,
> Come for a trip in my airship
> and we'll visit the man in the moon.

And when they walked down Waikawa Valley, as close to the moon as possible, they met the old maori running from the ghosts and he called out, Goodnight Miss Hefflin, only he said it like Heaven, and she laughed.

Perhaps Amy thinks for a moment of this, or is it only in books, where cried-for moons are captured, that they think this way?

And then the children are off to school and the littlest one plays in the backyard, that's Chicks, chicken because she's so small and dark; and Francie's there, who's not small but twelve, thirteen after Christmas, but left school now to make her way in the world and get on.

And be part of the day that is forever.

And it is quiet now for Francie. She thinks, now the girls at school will be marching in for prayers. A new term has begun. The headmistress will be standing on the platform and raise her hand, not for silence because it is hushed already but because she likes to raise her hand that way. She is big, with a head shaped like a bull and no neck to speak of and you can never see what she is wearing under her gown because it wraps her close like a secret. She is standing, in majesty, before the school and saying Good Morning, girls.

And then it is the National Anthem and the headmistress welcomes everybody for a new term, singing with them, or opening her mouth like singing,

> Lord Behold us with thy blessing
> once again assembled here
> onward be our footsteps pressing
> in thy love and faith and fear
> still protect us still protect us
> by thy presence ever near.

—The Lord, the headmistress says, after the Amen, is very very close.

And she wraps her gown more secretly about her body.

She opens the Bible then, and reads about the Sermon on the Mount.

—And seeing the multitudes he went up into a mountain.

—And, she says the Beatitudes. Blessed are the peacemakers and those that are poor in spirit and those that mourn, and how Christ taught them, saying.

They repeat then, the Lord's Prayer, not looking, with a special word added in case there is War, to make the soldiers not afraid; and they sing a long hymn, conducted by the music mistress who is deaf and lipreads and is related to Beethoven; and the hymn has so many verses that if it is a hot day some of the girls faint or have to walk out into the cool air and are able to boast about it afterwards,

—I fainted. I walked out of Assembly, when they sang the long hymn.

O give me Samuel's ear, they sing. His watch the little child the little Levite kept. A real watch, a ticking kind that slices and doles out day like best cake, or the looking watch that you live, sitting your life in a dark house like a box, in case an enemy should come?

It is a sad hymn, the little Levite one, and some of the girls, even the ones with two-storied homes and cars and caravans, will cry; yet when it is finished everything is school again, and the headmistress not any nearer to God; as if there had been no Bible or Jesus going up to the mountain where the air is cool, tasting of snowgrass that grows all the way up; and He passes a dead sheep that the hawks have eaten, and some live sheep sitting side-saddle upon the grass and chewing their cud. And it is a most beautiful mountain out of geography, a Southern Alp, but lessons never teach you how to write it; you only make shading like featherstitch.

So it is all gone in a cloud, and the headmistress is crossing her gown over her bosom and saying

—Girls, there were a number of navy coats and panama hats left at the end of last term. If no one claims them they shall be given to the Chinese Relief Fund.

—Girls, some of you have been seen in the street and not wearing gloves, or talking on corners to the boys from the High School. Girls, girls.

The headmistress is very stern.

The Invercargill March then, and soon the hall is empty.

And Francie is at home caught in a forever morning where every sound is loud and strange. The kitchen clock, the old one that belonged to her grandfather, ticks with a nobbly loudness, staring with its blank dark eye where you put the key to wind it. The front of the clock opens and inside are kept for safety, receipts and bills, art union tickets, and all things that must never be lost or the Withers will be up before the court or bankrupt.

Yet the clock is time, and time is lost, is bankrupt before it begins.

Francie sits in the kitchen. The fire burns with a hissing sound, then a roar until the damper is put in. Sometimes the coal makes a pop-pop.

—It's the gas, Mrs Withers explains. The coal we buy never has it, only the coal your father gets from work.

—Does he pay for it?

—No, Francie, he just brings home what we need.

The forever morning has a bird outside on the plum tree, a dog barking, the voice of the baker calling on the next door neighbour and saying,

—Did you get your bread at the weekend?

and the words seep through the holly hedge, are pricked on the way, come dropping through the kitchen window, firm and red words like holly berries and smelling like bread and primroses and the inside of a teapot.

And why, it *is* teatime, morning tea, and Mrs Withers is sitting spread out on the bin by the fire and drinking tea, with a home-made biscuit leaning wet to the waist in the saucer; and the tide rises and drowns the biscuit and she rescues it, though some of the soggy parts drop on the floor, and she dunks the remains in her tea. And the fairy ring of criss-cross that she made around the edge with an old knitting needle, for decoration, is crumbled away.

And still lunch time does not come. The world is stuck and over and over like a burning spinning and hurt record, and the world is empty,

a blue and white sack, hollow, with no people in it, save Mrs Withers and Chicks in a far corner

and the sack gets filled with a bird on the plum tree, and the baker saying

—Did you get your bread at the weekend?
and the clock making a stifling ticking that hops round and round droning, like a swarm, in the sack, and is never let free.

7

—Francie, Mr Withers said, will go to work at the Woollen Mills.

It was teatime. Poached eggs with pale yolks, bought from the store where the eggs are kidnapped from the hens and put in the dark and stamped on the shell with blue writing, and made valuable. The Withers own hens had stopped laying and though they gave them greens and let them have the run of the garden, and ground up oyster shells for them, the hens would not lay any more. They were retired hens. They made Bob Withers angry. He would go to shoo them in at night and they would sink before him with their wings outspread and their feet doubled up, in a kind of cramp, and not move, and Bob Withers would get angry and call them names, though not really bad names because the man who lived next door belonged to the Church, a missionary, who had been to the Islands, and was queer of course, for he sunbathed in the nude, and the children looked through at him. Their mother and father did not know they looked. Francie knew about him, but did not look, because she was left school and grown up and ready to make her way in the world; besides, she didn't need to look,

—I have plenty of opportunity, my dear Daphne, for looking at things like that.

—Tim Harlow, Daphne said.

And Francie hit her. Though as a matter of fact it *was* Tim Harlow, and Francie's parents were worried because Francie was, Mrs Withers said, a young woman ready to take her place in the world, and it was dangerous for her to be out with Tim Harlow, or any man. Why, Francie could get into trouble and be a disgrace to her parents and have to go away for a holiday up north while the baby came and everything was fixed up. And if the neighbours asked after her, Mrs Withers would be hard put to find an answer. She would have to say, swiftly,

—On holiday.

And then change the subject to how much cornflour to put in a sponge cake.

—So Francie, Mr Withers said, will go to work at the Woollen Mills.

Francie did not even wait to finish her poached egg or sop it up with bread and butter. She ran from the table and into the bedroom, crying when she reached there and no one could look.

Daphne followed her, but when she tried to open the bedroom door she found that Francie had fixed the back of a chair under the door handle.

—Let's in, Francie, she called.

Francie didn't answer. She was crying.

—Francie, let me in, you *have* to let me in, because I have a plan.

Francie opened the door and let Daphne in, then put the chair against the door.

—Why aren't they coming, she asked, to storm us?

—I suppose they're consulting. Francie, you *won't* go to work at the mill?

The two girls did not really know what the mill was, except that years ago small children had worked in mills, never seeing the sunlight for years, so that when they were rescued they turned blind, like pit ponies, and had to be led about on a leather strap that scarred them for the rest of their lives. The two girls knew little of Francie's mill. They knew that every morning at eight o'clock the mill made a scream like a fire siren and Francie and Daphne would look at each other and know that the mill girls had begun work. They rode bicycles, six abreast sometimes, though it was against the rules, along the main highway, going north, sometimes with the wind in their faces, riding on and on in the wind, with their permed hair going straggly unless it was covered with a gipsy scarf, and their coats flying open and their faces prepared and unsmiling; and leather lunch baskets strapped on the carrier of their bicycles, or money in their purse for pies at dinner-time from the nearby shop with the fly-specked window and the giant, dusty, and empty packets of Weetie and Kornie; and on the counter the jagged bright pink book of raffle tickets, the chance of a lifetime, first prize a washing machine and, consolation, a vacuum cleaner; riding on and on, the mill girls, with the mill out of sight and the girls driven there by a secret siren in their head, that sounded in triumph over the whole town when it had captured every particle of its prey. It seemed the mill girls rode into a nothing of north wind, or the nor'wester that choked them with hot dust from the plains; or some days spurred and chased by the wind from the south, off the snow, Francie's mother would say, and Francie and Daphne knew that over and over again the hundreds of girls, some Francie's age, were bewitched into a dark room filled with wool, where they were forced to fight their way through mounds of thick dusty-smelling bundles, grey and brown, green and gold, and blue like the sky that was shut out. Some of the girls choked with the colours and died.

Suddenly Francie, who had stopped crying, took off the top of her dress, it was a little coat striped like wallpaper, with small roses, and Aunty Nettie had made it. Francie looked at herself in the mirror.

—I am grown up, she said.

She had pink bulges where Daphne had mere tittie dots.

—I am grown up and I have left school because there is not enough money. Not many girls of my age have left school, have they Daphne? And not many been in the plannies with a boy, have they Daffy? And sent away for the free book on becoming an opera singer, have they Daffy?

Daphne could have hit her, she felt so wild with her for being grown up. She fixed the button on the front of her dress, so Francie couldn't see, and wiped over the mirror with her sleeve, to smooth away sight of herself and her thin chest and brown straight hair; but only breath was smoothed away, like frost, and she saw her face with its green eyes pick the pie looking at her. She turned to Francie,

—I've done some things you haven't. I am going to win some money and go to school and learn things that matter and not ever marry or die or be rich. I know Where the bee sucks, it is a song we have at school. Where the bee sucks there suck I.

—Oh, any old fool knows that song.

And Francie began to sing—
Where the bee sucks there suck I
In a cowslip's bell I lie;
There I couch when owls do cry.
When owls do cry, when owls do cry.

That is about a fairy spirit on a night in summer, a night like now, on the lawn by the japonica bush and the rose arch, but—Daffy?

—What Francie?

—I don't know.

—I don't know either.

And they both began to cry and hug each other, and then Francie stopped and blew her nose, shooting it out with one finger over her nostril the way her father did, and it landed on the mirror. She wiped it off.

—Do you really think Dad will send me to the mill?

Daphne tried to say something kind to her, something kind and futile the way their mother said when their uniform was creased and it was a quarter to nine and no time to put the iron on the stove.

—The creases will come out in the air, kiddies.

Oh kind air that never could fulfil any promise.

So Daphne said mysteriously to Francie,

—You never know what strange things may happen.

There came to them both, then, a red and gold and black thought, and they looked at each other and spoke it.

—A bicycle.

—with a dynamo.

—tail light

—headlight

—painted red, painted gold painted black

—a pump lying along the bar

—a carrier

—a bag of tools fastened with a shiny silver dome thing,

—handbrake

—footbrake, bell

—no free-wheeler.

—no, brakes. Or you'll go over the handlebars downhill and be like Ted West and wear a black patch over your eye till you're dead.

And oh, oh to cycle in the wind, they thought.

8

The next morning Mr Withers went down to Joe Clevely's, on the way to work, and bought a lady's bicycle, ten shillings down and five shillings a week. When he collected it afterwards he was afraid to ride it in case it broke, so he wheeled it home. Certainly, he thought, the girl will have to have a bicycle to ride to the mill, and it's easier time payment than straight cash for second-hand. But he was afraid of the bicycle. He was afraid of all new things, not the trifles you buy and pay for and take home to call your own, and don't have to fill in forms about, and promise; but the big things like bicycles and lawn-mowers where you sign a paper, in case. And the newness of the bicycle shone, for him, like a conscience, with every touch of his dirty coal- and oil-stained hands, making a dark brand that nothing would seem to erase, and where was the money coming from, that was the question, where was the money coming from?

When Daphne came home from school Francie was standing at the gate to meet her. Leaning on her bicycle, feeling the cold black shiny bars. She rang the bell, for Daphne to hear. The sound turned and sliced the air like a new metal windmill. She let Daphne ring the bell, too. Then

—Come for a ride, she said.

And Daphne threw her books inside the gate by the japonica bush and they went out in the street, riding in the wind, with the houses melting like lumps of fat, white and red lumps stuck upon a wide wide silver plate of world where they rode, Daphne and Francie, in the north wind that said, Rain, and in the south wind that said, in the poem,

We shall have snow.

Snow.

Francie and Daphne were riding in colours, red and gold and black, a shiny secret black, firm and to be filled, like the gloss of a dark new shoe; yet at the back of the wind coming in their faces there lay an opposite world of snow, no colour, that would creep nearer, first in a breath of south wind, then in a storm they could not see or understand, that would cover them with flakes, like lace, and they would be swathed in lace, though never warm like in their grandma's black shoe-shiny breast where she kept her lace hanky tucked and curled like a cosy feather; only cold lace; they would sleep at night in cold lace. In the morning they would get up and taking tiny shovels they would gather up all the snow that lay around them, in their hair and eyes, and they would struggle and cry out, and nothing would save them.

The South wind doth blow
and we shall have snow.

9

The next night, at teatime, Bob Withers asked for
everyone to be quiet. He wanted to speak. He asked by
thumping his fist on the table so that the cups and saucers
jumped a little with the shock.
—The woman down the road, Mrs Mawhinney, wants someone to help with the housework. I said Francie would go
   down. She'll get about a pound a week, I think. Or more.
   They're a family that's pretty well off, just her and the two
   girls going to High.
—But Dad, the Mill, my bicycle!
Francie now would have striven every day with armies of
wool in order to cycle back and forth in the north and south
wind, why for nights she and Daphne had lain in bed imagining what would happen. They understood now, why the mill
girls took tickets in the wonderful raffle, the washing machine
and vacuum cleaner and hair-drier; it was to have these things
sitting in their head, like a charm, to magic away the drudgery
and blindness, the way the bicycle would magic for Francie,
and knowing about the south wind. Daphne had arranged to
pray for her when she entered the factory and when the mill
siren sounded she was to say a special charm, from the fairy-
tale book, so that Francie would not be captured for ever but
have some of her old Francie left; and so that her arms would
not tire and ache in her struggle with wool and being drowned
in red and gold and blue the way a swimmer struggles with
seaweed, outside the flags, in Friendly Bay or the world, and
is pulled under.
The wool had become real, a being that threaded and tangled
its way through their waking and dreaming lives, and now
here was their father coming to cut their monstrous dream
and murder their so loved and longed-for fear. And Francie,
Francie would never now cycle back and forth in the wind,
as a reward for fighting the wool; it would not any more be
like the fairy-tale where the hero will kill his enemy and win
worlds of gold, a fair woman, a mountain of jewels.

And Daphne had thought, Francie will go along the north road, and if it is autumn and there are flocks of birds in the paddocks, to pick at the thistledown and cocksfoot or ride on the stalks of grass, all the gold finches will follow Francie in a cloud, to protect her; and if it is near winter the wax-eyes hungry for honey, will make their green and yellow cloud to follow her. Daphne had thought.

—Yes, what about my bicycle, Dad?

—You can still have it. You'll be able to pay for it yourself. It'll do you good to work. Now you've left school you can't hang around home the way you've been doing, you've got to make your way in the world.

Everything in the room was quiet when Mr Withers spoke. The kettle was knocking and panting but Mrs Withers didn't dare get up to see to it, or put a new shovel of dull coal on the fire. The children, Francie and Daphne, and then the youngest, Chicks, with black hair, and the boy Toby, with his head hanging on one side and his eyes in a cloud of dream, sat still, looking at their father and his shadow that was cut in two, lying across the edge of the table and then sitting up against the wall and across the calendar that told the day of the month and when the bills were due and the rent and the electric light; and lying across the table, his shadow had the shape of a fern, like the one he wore in his coat for he was a returned soldier and had been gassed in the war, the First War, there are too many wars and it is all money and putting things down on the bill and making your way in the world, and taking hold, like the mill girls, of the wrong magic and the wrong fairy-tale.

And listening to their father say about Francie, the children felt afraid, as if suddenly the walls of the house would collapse and the roof disappear and leave them, naked, with nothing to shut them away from the world, and the world in one stride would walk in and take possession of them, holding them tight in its hand of rock and lava, as if they were insects, and they would have to struggle and kick and fight to escape and make their way. And each time they made their way and the world had dropped them for a while to a peaceful hiding place, it would again seize them with a burning one of its million hands, and the struggle would begin again and again and go on and on and never finish.

10

Francie started the following Monday at Mawhinney's. It was just down the road, not ever far enough for her to ride her bicycle and have green and gold birds in her hair. And even having a bicycle, like having a mountain of jewels or a magic ring, did nothing to help Francie just as nothing can ever help. She went by herself to a house filled with rooms and carpets that soaked up footsteps like coloured moss; and a widow, Mrs Mawhinney, in a black dress like a monk; and the two girls, one with a broken leg and a wooden crutch worn almost soft as a pillow where the girl, Ruby, leant her arm to walk; and the other girl, Doris, saying whenever she felt surprised, and she seemed always surprised,

—Oh Snakes. Oh Snakes.

Francie had put on her lipstick that she had found in the grass by the reserve, and she wore an old coat that Aunty Nettie had sent with the parcel of things that

—May come in handy for the girls.

—Goodbye. Daphne sang out after her.

—Goodbye, Francie said.

And she added, in the same voice that women in films use when they dismiss their lovers for the last time,

—Goodbye, *schoolgirl*.

Daphne did not know Francie after that. Francie was secret. She bought a pair of grey slacks and went down town in them, on a Sunday too, and Bob Withers, who did not go to Church but knew what people thought, tried to thrash Francie for wearing slacks on a Sunday and being a disgrace; but he couldn't. She was grown up.

—They all wear them, nowadays, Francie said.

And their father looked bewildered and did not know what to do, and said to his wife,

—The girl needs discipline.

And he said he would burn the slacks under the copper or send Francie to the Industrial School, and that Francie was getting like the woman down the road, who ran wild, having parties every Saturday night with housey-housey and drink. And their father was frightened, and every time he saw the slacks he got angry, but not, now, at Francie, only at her mother. He seemed to get angrier every day, and more frightened, and the bills kept coming in one on top of the other.

—The bill's more than it should be this week, he would say.

And Amy Withers would go red and say that the chocolate biscuits were for Aunty Nettie passing through on the Limited, that she had a sweet tooth and you could never get anything at the refreshment rooms except a bun stuffed with a dirtyfoam of cream, or a stale sandwich, or a pie, and that made Aunty Nettie bilious, and spoilt the journey.

And Francie's father would pick at something else, the way someone who is knitting will pull at the threads to make a hole, but their father tried to pick and unpick something inside himself that every year of being alive had knitted, with the pattern, the purl and plain of time gone muddled and different from the dream neatness.

But Francie seemed happy. One day she had her photo taken in the slacks. She was walking along the street when a man stopped her and handed her a ticket with a number on it, and it turned out he had taken a photo of her in slacks. When the photo was developed she showed it to Daphne, who said,

—You look as if you have been crying.

And perhaps Francie had, perhaps she was not as happy as it seemed.

Daphne and Francie didn't sleep together any more, though they used the same mirror for making faces and smiling in and trying on in front of. Francie had the front room. And she treated her bicycle as if it were ordinary. And she didn't talk much. Mrs Mawhinney gave her an evening dress with holey black lace along the hem and Francie went to a dance—a hop she called it—and she didn't tell Daphne everything about it, because, she said

—You wouldn't understand.

—But I would understand, I would, Francie, honest I would. Tell me.

But Francie looked far away and said

—All right, Daphne, as between women I'll tell you. You won't be shocked?

—I'll never, never be shocked. I wasn't shocked when you told me about the postman and Mae West, was I?

Yet Francie changed her mind and refused to tell. She said she had danced, and she thought she was expert at doing the military two-step; though she liked the maxina better. She said the names of the dances proudly, the way some people mention the names of friends and relations they are proud to know,

—My uncle, the bank manager.

—My cousin, who's gone overseas.

—But, Francie said, of all dances I like best the destiny, which means fate. That is, if you have the right partner. Do you know anything, by the way, about heartbeats?

Daphne said no because she knew she was expected to say no.

—Well, if you're dancing with the right partner, your heart beats in time with his. You can feel his heart, and he can feel yours. They thump on each other.

—Like two tennis balls knocking, I suppose?

—Something like, only different.

Then Francie turned her face sideways, for she liked her profile view better than front on, and she wrung her hands and looked tragic, yet aloof and indifferent, and said,

—But you wouldn't really understand, you can't until you've been through what I've been through. I've suffered. We all suffer, from the heart, and then you say the heart's like a tennis ball.

—I meant the thumping and bouncing.

—The heart, Francie said, is like a globe of fire.

And that was all she told Daphne about the dances, and would answer no questions about being taken home and getting kissed.

Though sometimes at night, the time for confidences, when even the pink-footed mouse is less afraid, and the hedgehog uncurled and sniffling along in the grass and leaves outside, and inside warm with no hurricane of world to threaten the walls of the house, Daphne and Francie would sit together on the old sofa in Francie's room, and try to talk about everything and the world and being grown-up and having a husband and children and a house with a front doorstep to be scrubbed and the lace curtains to be washed; and the garden with its laid green rope of vegetables, the cabbages with their pants tucked above their knees like the young rooster in the fowl-yard; and the carrots growing lacy and siamese; and the hedge high in case the neighbours looked in to see; and the babies coming, and the mothers talking over the fence to the neighbours and comparing, comparing—

and everything,
and everything.

One night, it was the last night Francie ever talked much about being grown-up, she said to Daphne,

—Do you know what?

—What?

—You know Easter time and the eggs and silver paper and that? Well, when we're children we eat the eggs straight away, don't we? But if you're grown up you keep them. It's the same with chocolates, and anything nice.

—How do you know?

—Because of Mawhinney's. Their front room is filled with Easter eggs that Mrs Mawhinney hasn't even bothered to take the paper off.

—Why?

—I don't know. When you're grown up, you're frightened to taste the nice things, like Easter eggs, in case you never get them again, or something, so you save them up till you have rooms full of them. It's like spending money and being afraid because you've spent it; only this isn't money, it's something inside people that they're afraid to spend. I know, from Mawhinney's and other places. And then you die, and leave yourself and the nice things wrapped up, like an Easter egg, with the lovely wavery paper still on it, and the black patterned chocolate inside. I know. I think grown-ups are silly.

They agreed that grown-ups were silly.

—But you have to grow up. It's today and tomorrow and the next day.

And it came with Francie—today and tomorrow and the next day. She grew more and more silent about what really mattered. She curled inside herself like one of those black chimney brushes the little shellfish you see on the beach, and you touch them, and they go inside and don't come out.

And every day when Francie went to work, walking the few yards down the road to Mawhinney's, she seemed to be going miles away. And Daphne thought, one time when she peeped through the hedge at Francie going, If only she had some kind of treasure with her, inside, to help her; if only grown-ups could tell what is treasure and not treasure
    if only
like the bicycle made magic and the gold and green clouds

of birds to help her fight the armies of tangled wool, oh it was all tangled, being alive was tangled, and there was Francie going by herself every day to face it and fight it.

What if she were caught and choked and never came back?

11

All sun. The ripening fruit of sky bleeding, band-aged with snow-skin of autumn cloud; the noon light dripping from the trees in gold flakes called leaves; the four poplars at the corner, high-up, atwitch with trickle of air down the funnel of light from hill to valley, hill to valley—drop of air sharp as a buried crocus blade, sweet upon the poplar leaf as words of curse from the mad woman, Minnie Cuttle.

And the old old shuffle of decay.

It was Saturday afternoon. Over the hedge from the Withers the lawnmower spitting out grass and the smell in the air and the green stain on old Bill Flett's boots and on Phyllis Flett's hands, playing with the grass, fistful, and smelling it with no one to throw it at, only big brothers, away where?

Football, soccer, running round the block in spiked shoes for the Amateur Athletic Society, sitting in the gardens with a girl friend, or walking on the Marine Parade, looking at the sea, throwing stones at it,

—I want to throw something, I want to hit something, I want to *do* something.

—What, Eddie Flett?

—I don't know. Something big. Kiss me, Marge.

—Not here, Eddie, with everyone looking, and the kids on the merry-go-round, and that couple on the seat.

The green seat like a washingboard where the sea scrubs its pink fingernails.

—Come in here, Phyllis, away from the grass.

No lawnmower now, it must be nearly afternoon tea time.

The Withers children dangling, doing nothing, caught in the scruff of the neck by afternoon; looking through the fence at the Fletts who are Catholic dogs and stink like frogs and eat no meat on

Fri-i-i-i-day.

Then, let's to the rubbish dump, the children cry.

So there was Francie to look after them, to help Toby if he took a fit, and put a piece of stick in his mouth to keep him from biting his tongue, and lay him somewhere warm with a coat over him while he slept. And Francie to see they all stopped now and again for Chicks to catch up, because Chicks was smallest. And Francie to boss Daphne, and not let her be boss, it was one or the other.

And they went to the rubbish dump to look for treasure.

Francie wore her slacks, with zipp at the side and a pocket, and her hand in her pocket, also a sixpenny shout from her pay for blackballs or acid drops or aniseed balls, it was toss up which. Daphne wore her tartan jacket, no particular tartan, that Aunty Nettie had sent in the last parcel, and her navy skirt with the petersham she had put on herself, after the last sewing class. And Chicks wore a red spotted dress, up over her knees. And Toby his navy pants and flannel shirt and braces.

But it doesn't matter what they wore, not like at a wedding, or if they were being described for the newspapers, it's just so you can see them and know which is which—

Francie, Toby, Daphne, Chicks Withers going to find treasure and knowing they would find it; the same way that grown-up people (they thought) go to shops and offices and factories, what they call their work, to find their grown-up treasure.

It wasn't far for the Withers children to go. Over the hill and down and then along to Cross Street. All the way there were people working in their gardens, mowing the lawn or digging; and ladies, on little rubber mats, kneeling over primrose plants and pansies. And all the way there were houses with lace curtains looped in front, and ornaments, dogs and frogs looking out of the window and being so surprised, perhaps, to see Francie, Toby, Daphne, Chicks on their way to the rubbish dump to look for treasure.

They met Tim Harlow riding round and round on his bicycle. He stopped to talk to Francie.

—Gidday, cutie.

Francie put her head in the air and walked on, quickly, then she turned round and smiled at him. He smiled back.

—The cheek he's got, Francie said proudly.

—Are you going with him? Daphne said.

—Never, said Francie. Never put all your eggs in one basket.

Besides, he's younger. Oh look, a dead hedgehog.

It was lying squashed and dead in the middle of the road.

—Why, asked Chicks, coming up behind.

Francie explained.

—At night, she said, the hedgehogs think that because it is dark they can come out and walk quite safely, and what better place to walk than a road, tarsealed with a white line running down the middle.

She was joking. She knew Tim Harlow was not far behind, and she was proud and joking. It was like Francie to do that, to joke when they came to something sick or dead, because she was growing up quickly and getting to know things, and left school to earn her living and what were hedgehogs, anyway.

So she said,

—It's nothing, leave it. Don't touch it with your clean hanky, Daphne. When I get married and have a car I shall probably run over hundreds and hundreds of hedgehogs without even knowing it. They're a blot on the landscape.

Daphne withdrew her hanky. After all, the hedgehog was dead and thát was sad, but it was a squashed and dirty kind of death that made you turn your face away.

They came to the rubbish dump, the stink and filth of it, with the toi-toi like a fringe of shawl; and they climbed over grass and dead logs and twisted iron, and sat together on a clean piece, cocksfoot and no ashes, for a rest and to take the gravel out of Chick's shoe. There was no real leaning-place so they sat upright with their knees up and their elbows on their knees. They compared knees.

—Yours are nobbly, they said to Toby.

Toby didn't talk much. He just got angry and threw things, or he cried. He looked at his nobbly knees and then at Chicks because she was smaller and couldn't argue so well.

—Yours are nobbly knees, too.

—I have got webbed fingers, Daphne said, spreading out her hands. Which proves I am part fish.

—I have a wart, to put plantain on, Francie said. Then she sighed and shrugged her shoulders.

—What children you are, it's a wonder I can bear to look after you on a Saturday when I *could* be doing all kinds of interesting things with certain friends of mine. What did we come here for, anyway? I'm sure I'm not going to sit here all day in a dirty old rubbish dump.

—But, Francie, you used to come with us, before.

—Before what?

—Before you left school and everything was different.
Wouldn't you like to be at school again, and Joan of Arc.
She was a Saint.

Francie giggled.

—Saints are not in my line. And I'd much rather be grown
up. Tell you what, though, let's go down over there where
they're burning things, and watch. For half an hour, mind
you, then we're going home, and we're getting acid drops
and *not* aniseed balls on the way home.

Chicks started to cry. She hadn't really wanted to come to
the dump, for it was a long way to walk and have to catch up
all the time, but Francie had said aniseed balls, and all the
way Chicks had been imagining them, brown in the mouth
first, then white with a tiny blue rim or shadow, then pure
white like a warm hailstone.

—But you said aniseed balls, Francie.

—Did I? How fascinating. Well threepence-worth of each,
then, and no more snivelling.

They went over to see the fire. It was bigger than they
thought, and smoky, with the smell of petrol and kerosene
and rubber and stifled rags. There was a man guarding it,
thrashing it with a bag to subdue it, and sometimes poking
it with a stick to make it flame. He turned to the children
standing at the top of the hollow.

—Get away you kids or you'll be blown up, or burned.

Francie stared at him. Why, she thought, it's Tim Harlow's
father. And he said his father was a surgeon in his spare time,
performing operations and wearing rubber gloves and masks
of gauze, and having the sweat wiped off him by nurses as
pretty as me, and everything handed to him. And he's only a
Council man. She moved closer to look at him.

And then no one can describe exactly what happened, but
it happened, and Francie tripped over a rusty piece of plough
and fell headfirst down the slope, rolling, quickly, into the
flames. And Tim Harlow's father, the Council man, tried to
grab her, and leapt high, like a ballet dancer, to reach her,
crying as he danced,

—Help, help, or get a doctor, or help!

His sack shadowed red from the flames that he danced to

and dared, like a matador; beating in the air and on the ground.

And Daphne and Toby and Chicks ran forward, calling out,

—Francie, Francie, Francie, as if her name, three times said, would bring her alive, like magic.

—For God's sake, yelled Mr Harlow.

And he grabbed hold of the children and thrust them back. And people came from everywhere, like an ambush, and there was a woman tearing up a sheet and it was Mrs Peterson from the Plunket, and she was flat and dark, like a blackboard, with horror chalked on her face. And Daphne and Toby and Chicks were taken over the road to Harlow's and given a drink of hot milk and a piece of seed cake, to wait for a car to take them home. And they sat on a sofa that had a dusty piece of stuffing bursting from its middle, like the inside of a dead hedgehog.

They sat in a row, with their legs dangling because the sofa was too high and they held tight to their piece of seedcake, but they didn't eat it, and it got squashed with being held, and warm, and the crumbs dropped on Harlow's carpet; but nobody minded. Mrs Harlow, who was a light woman, curved like a feather, with hair yellow like toi-toi, looked in the door at them. She had a piece of seedcake in her hand and seemed not to know where to put it. She looked quickly round the room as if to find someone to give the seedcake to, but there was no one else there but Daphne, Toby and Chicks; so she put the cake in a dish, beside a packet of needles and a wad of darning wool, and the seedcake sprouted into a tall gold flower growing up through the roof and further than the sky, and Daphne saw it, and picked one of its petals to take home in the car.

—There's a car coming soon, soon, my dears, said Mrs Harlow. Now drink up your milk and eat your seedcake, why the littlest one's nearly asleep and so pale, the poor little mite.

And they sat for years and years on the sofa till it grew dark outside or seemed to be dark, there must have been something wrong with the sun, yet it wasn't dark really, for when Daphne looked sideways out of the window there it was, daylight, with the sun out, and the street with the cars going up and down tooting their horns, and little dogs hopping about, and people walking. And the mist coming on the window, a dampness in the air that made people take their washing from the clothes-line, and button their coats and collars.

And then Daphne looked back into the room where they sat, in the dark. There was the tall sideboard with the dish of fruit on one side, apples, an orange, a banana going bad; and on the other side, the darning wool and the seedcake in flower. And a gold plate with a deer in a forest painted on it; and on the wall a picture of dogs, four of them, with their noses in the air and their tails up, and a man on horseback beside them, a hunting picture.

And so they sat still and not speaking, until Toby's hand shook and his teeth chattered and it was a fit; and Daphne had to do what was Francie's job, though it made her feel sick, fixing his mouth and letting him have more room on the sofa to lie down. And nobody came in the room for many years then, and it seemed they had been put inside there to sit still and grow staying there without seeing any more people or going home.

Home?

Years after, a man came in a car and took them home.

12

Mrs Withers disapproved of two kinds of people, insurance men and travelling salesmen. She had heard stories about them, and once, when the family had been living in the deep south where old grandma Withers toiled in the cotton fields as a negress, an insurance man had put his foot in the door, and Mrs Withers shut fast the door on his foot, nearly squeezing it in two, and squeezed feet are very painful, as people know, from their own new shoes, and from the faces of all the people who tried to fit the slipper left by Cinderella.

—I told you, nothing today, thank you, Mrs Withers repeated, jamming the door harder in case the insurance man needed any more proof.

No, she disapproved of them. Rooks, hounds, she called them. Bloodsuckers. Though really what they sucked was money which seems, however, to be another form of blood necessary for life.

So the day the children went off to the rubbish dump and a man, like an insurance agent though it was Saturday, knocked at the back door, Amy Withers put her sack apron on the bench in the scullery and opened the door, just a little, then jammed it fast, for she knew the man was a salesman.

—Nothing today, thank you, she said. I cannot afford it.

The man was obstinate and put his foot in the door.

—I've come, he said.

Amy would not let him finish.

—Nothing today thank you. I cannot possibly buy whatever you have to sell.

The man smiled sadly, then pushed suddenly at the door, and walked in. He said he was a doctor and didn't want to sell anything. He thought, as he entered the depressing and untidy kitchen, it's a commercial world, certainly, where even death is bought and sold, and the world is bankrupt in death.

—No, he said aloud, he didn't want to sell anything.

But he sold death, the terrible way, on the never-never, though Amy tried to keep him out.

He told about Francie, and said

—Pull yourself together, Mrs Withers. I take it your husband is up north with the Limited. He'll be home any time now. He knows, but he doesn't know the details yet.

And when Bob Withers came home, with his workbag of coal in one hand, and his dirty blueys in the other, and his face puckered he stood in the doorway and saw Amy sitting in the corner on the bin, with her arm around Chicks, and the other children standing around and pale, and the kitchen fire out.

He kissed his wife and started to cry and his overalls dropped on the floor and unrolled into the empty stained pattern of his other work-self, flat and robbed.

—Oh Bob, Amy said. You're home early. You've never been home early before.

The children had never seen their father cry before. They had thought that fathers get angry and shout about the bills and wearing slacks, and laugh with the woman from the bookstall, and sometimes with mothers; but never cry.

He looked like a bird, with his mouth down at the corners, the way a fowl looks when the rest of the fowls have been put in for the night, and the realisation of their going has overtaken the last fowl; and she panics; and her beak drops; and that is how Bob Withers face seemed when he really knew about Francie. He knew later than the others. They had been warned, and driven, like fowls at night, inside, though not to warmth. Driven inside to outerness, as if the moment they passed through the door of knowing, they came, not to warm nests, but dropped down to dark, yet in some kind of comfort because they were together and close; and there was Bob waiting to be driven inside to share the darkness of their complete knowing, and not wanting to go, and being scared, like the lost fowl.

Francie did not come home that night to sleep in the bed in the front room. Although Daphne knew she was dead, she expected her to come and do her hair in front of the mirror and pull her dress tight around her waist, to see her measurement, if she were slim enough; and stand kicking her legs up, acting like a chorus girl; and practising her grand opera, though the free book had cheated and was not free and you had to pay twenty guineas for learning opera. And then squeezing out her blackheads, the ones in the seam of her nose and cheek. And plucking her eyebrows. Daphne expected all this, but it did not happen. Instead, the tweezers that Francie used for plucking stayed in exactly the same place on the duchesse. They stayed there for hours and days and weeks. Once, Daphne moved them a few inches to see what they were like moved, if they looked any different. And she went to the wardrobe and jiggled the clothes up and down, danced the evening dress backward and forward, though it had nobody inside it, danced it, the destiny and maxina, just to see. If only she could have seen! Just once more, only once, and then it wouldn't matter.

And through it all Amy Withers said,
—Have faith.

Through the funeral and the flowers and the cards that she put in a cane shopping basket, shaped like a cradle; to be gone through afterwards and the nicest ones picked out to keep, the ones with the white gloss on them and the raised cross entwined with flowers, and words to tell that Francie was not really dead, only sleeping. Through it all, Amy Withers said,
—Have faith.

You could not see faith, but it was somewhere to help, like the air that was to uncrease the school tunics; so, now, when the pattern of life had become unpleated and disarranged, it was, for Amy Withers.

Faith will smooth everything.

And also seeing Francie on resurrection day.

13

The long corridor outside shines like the leather of a new shoe that walks that walks upon itself in a ghost footstep upon its own shining until it reaches the room where the women wait, in night clothes, for the nine o'clock terror called electric shock treatment. They wear dressing gowns of red flannel, as if God or the devil had purchased a continent of cloth and walked, with scissors for stick, from coast to coast, to cut the dead mass pattern of mad men and women whose eyes will spring blind with sight of their world and the flag of cloth hung in the shape of sun across their only sky.

Oh, but at nine o'clock, it is said, all will be well. Their seeing will be blinded, the shade replaced across their eyes to restrict their looking to their plate, their tea, their cigarette; in practice for the world; stopped like a house to look forever on its backyard.

Hairclips have been taken from them and arranged in rows along the mantelpiece. Their teeth are sunk in handleless cups of luke-warm water, arranged in circles, for companionship, upon the bony-legged table.

—Take your teeth out, the women in pink have commanded. Take your teeth out.

And soon the same god or devil who walked the continent of cloth will turn the switch that commands—See. Forget. Go blind.

Be convulsed and never know why.

Take your teeth out as a precaution against choking, your eyes out, like Gloucester, to save you sight of the cliff and the greater gods who keep their 'dreadful pother' above your head. Your life out as a precaution against living.

And the women, submitting their teeth, their eyes, their lives, smile, embarrassed or mad in their world of mass red flannel.

The nurse is pink, like a flower from the garden, except the wind that bends her body is blown from the same continent of swamp and trapped water with the voice of God or the devil in her ear, like the same small voice that drove the horse, said Gee-up, Whoa.

on the sunniest of days, coloured like a single toi-toi with a sunflower in its heart of seedcake though the seeds were burned

black in ash that the same wind that bends and crushes the
pink body of flower had driven on and on through a million
years to a world of blindness

this room

and a black blanket laid like an elasticised and bordered
beetle upon the bed, and the women lying upon its furred shell
with their temples washed clean in a purple gasp of liquid
ethereal soap

concealed in cotton wool. And the gabbling jibbering forest-
quiet women wait in crocodile for the switch that abandons
them from seeing

and fear

and no struggle to leave for in seeing they inhabit a room
of blind where doors are moulded lockless, and those who
enter from the corridor may cleave the wall with their bodies,
and the same wall closes behind them in a velvet mass like a
wave in the wake of a journeying saint or ship.

But God or the devil has come, walking the long corridor,
squeezing his mind and voice in molecular drops through the
forbidding encircling wall. He greets the women. He wrings
the blood from their gowns of flannel. It drips upon the floor
into a creek flowing to the wall and not passing through and
now it is a wave pressing upon the wall and unable to escape.

The women scream. They fear drowning. Or burning.

The nurse picks off one of her pink petals, flutters it upon
the wave to soak the crimson, suck it in one breath. Then she
readjusts her body, tucking the petal in the gap between her
mouth and eyes, and smiles upon God or the devil who stands
ready to signal her with a lift of the hand, a widening of his
eyes, a signal as secretive as a scream

and the head of the writhing crocodile is broken off, dragged
through the door at the end of the room,

and the door flings itself open like two palms which gesture,
 Cela m'est egal, Cela m'est egal.

And the writhing head is borne inside, and the women
waiting hear a shuffle of footsteps, a voice, two voices, the
scream of a soul being surprised in a funnel of dark. Then
silence. Till the door flings itself open again in a gesture of
indifference, revealing its wooden hands and the grains of
heart and life and fate.

Cela m'est egal, cela m'est egal, it speaks like a carefree breath
or commonplace, and the wheeled-out bed holds what is left

of the head of the crocodile, whose face is blue, like Toby, with a black pipe like a whistle stuck in its mouth.

Its eyes are open in their triumph of instilled blindness.

Unconscious, the head groans and writhes and quickly, as it would die, it is screened by roses from the rest of the writhing crocodile, and its eyes closed and smoothed with the forefinger of the pink flower, gently, as the dead are treated, who cannot be hurt now; and the pipe taken from its mouth as if, had it lain longer there, it may have played too enticingly its melody of blindness.

And once more the crocodile is severed, the same procession to the door, the same quietness,

Cela m'est egal.

And now Daphne passes the rows of women who lie dead, each with her pipe or whistle thrust in her mouth, or quickly withdrawn in case the music make immobile, as in the fairy tale, the world outside and here.

The doors receive. The same indifference.

And God or the devil on the left, at the head of the raised bed that floats, chequered, like a shadow projected from the tethered real by some invisible globe of light. The doctor moves, carefully, as if he tiptoed between swords. He is guarding something. At first it seems his life. Then it is the machine, cream, with curved body and luminous eyes, one red, the dangerous eye, the other black for cancellation of impulse. He stands with his hand resting lightly, it seems lightly, upon his treasure; then Daphne knows he dare not move his hand away from the voluptuous body of the red and black-eyed machine which, in case of escape, is fastened, as a lover secures the object of his love with cords of habit, circumstance, convenience, time, with black charged cords, varicose, converging to a unity that is controlled by a switch, and pressure of the doctor's own hand.

—Turn on, my love, he will say, and reach for the switch, and caress the red luminous eye with his gentle hand.

He looks at Daphne, as if she may have interrupted his pleasure, or as if he will communicate to her, then blot from her knowing, the delight he feels in his lovely machine.

—Climb up on the bed, Daphne.

She climbs a suspended shadow of mountain and finds on its summit a golden hollow, her own size, for lying in. How well it fits, carved for her comfort, by each year of her life, changed to rain and wind from the north, or the south, bringing snow.

—Lie down, Daphne.

Daphne lies down. Suddenly over the top of the mountain, their heads level with the lowest cloud, there appear the faces, set and shaped in cloud, of five women dressed in white, envying the gold hollow. They look down and smile, to win friendship. Their hands itch to dig the gold, store it in their ample linen pockets and crawl from the room; for they *must* crawl, they are white insects with feelers waving in their heads, each feeler tipped with a trace of white like a separated snowdrop. They wave their feelers.

—Lie down, Daphne.

—Lie down, Daphne.

The doctor comes as close as he dare without drawing his hand from the switch of his love.

—Hello.

He smiles, a wicked deceitful smile, like the world after the morning, that reveals the truth of the golden mountain, of every gold mountain; that all are nests of clay, and the sun an inarticulate rock whose deceptive attribute of light, chipped off by pick-pick of time, closes upon the silence of its unshadow and oblivion.

—Hello, Daphne.

The women wave their feelers. They suddenly go stiff, their knees set like concrete, their breasts of stone; and press icicles upon Daphne's ears, and her body down, down in the hollow; though one of them says kindly,

—Put this in your mouth.

It is not an aniseed ball or acid drop or blackball, but a little black pipe or whistle.

—Bite it.

Should it not be played? Drop thy pipe, thy happy pipe.

The doctor, waiting, exults. He presses the switch. One moment then, and nothing.

14

Oh the wind is lodged forever in the telegraph wire for crying there on a grey day on the loneliest of roads of dust and gravel and forest of cocksfoot at the side and gorse

or broom hedge with the dead pods refusing to drop and the
cross the crucifix of the leaning poles linked by the everlasting
wire of crying of the wind lodged forever in the telegraph
wire for crying there.
The green baize and oil sickening smell of the gramophone
horn, a smell swallowed and vomited from memory upon a
folded sheet of summer, burned and boiled in a pumice copper
with a pine cone gum log, old apple wood.
Francie, come in you naughty bird
the rain is pouring down,
What would your mother say
if you stay there and drown?
You are a very naughty bird,
you do not think of me,
I'm sure I do not care,
said the sparrow on the tree.
Francie, come in you naughty bird, the rain is pouring down,
the fire is pouring down. Now be careful kiddies, for wherever
you walk you may meet an angel; for angels walk upon the
earth among people, and the day Christ comes He too will
walk unknown upon the earth. And blessed are the poor
in spirit for theirs is the kingdom of heaven.
Lay not up for yourselves treasures upon earth.
Blessed are they that mourn for they shall be
comforted, blessed are the pure in heart, for they shall see God.
And childhood is nothing, it is only the wind in the telegraph
wire for crying there, the toothache in the cavity of night,
the too big body curled up in the cot too small, the
grandmother breaking her back in the hot Virginny sun,
grandmother what big eyes you have; and the boy in the
fox's belly, unstitch, unstitch, boy girl or day locked in the
suffocating belly of memory.

Now that Francie is dead, I, Daphne, am the eldest sister,
the eldest in the family, not counting Toby who takes fits and
lies sometimes in hospital with his lips lolling together like
rubber and covered with saliva and his face twisted and his
eyes bulged. He does not know us when we go there at visiting
time, and the nurse leads us along a corridor to a room like a
cage, with bars, where Toby lies on a high bed white and
clean as a china plate; as high as the bed where the princess
lay, under twenty mattresses; the *real* princess. Toby, when you

get better we will go to the rubbish dump and find things. A diamond. A lump of gold. A moa bone. Toby we *must* find things that other people have thrown away as no use, all day and night they are standing on the edge of the cliff and throwing, and sometimes in the night they cannot see what they throw; in the night or sleep or dream; till they wake too old and late.

Toby when you come from hospital and they have paid the bills—but they will never pay the bills. The window letter will come from the hospital board and our mother will put it inside the clock or pin it to the calendar, and our father will reach for it when he comes home at night, hold it up to the light to read through and be prepared, then slit it open and throw up his hands or dance out of rage, like Rumpelstiltskin, though not going through the floor, and cry

—Money! Money!

And a little mouse will crawl from a hole in the corner of the bin and whisper, in a voice like hundreds and thousands, Money? In the bin we keep old shoes and books and pieces of leather that our father uses for mending. Where's the last, he calls out. Who has seen the last, and the hammer, and the box of tacks? And men in peaked blue caps come at night to help him mend our shoes.

Oh. Toby. Our father doesn't wear glasses to mend. He can see quick as light in the dark corners, or quick as the troutlet that moves to hide under the river-bank, its belly to the earth. So perhaps our father is not going blind yet. You remember Grandad wore glasses and pushed them up on top of his forehead as if there, in that shiny spot before you got to his hair, the shiny spot that in old people and babies gets covered with scales, again like fish, was a secret pair of eyes that needed help with looking. The case he kept his glasses in was rubbed and shiny too, with orange spots. Were they polka dots? What are polka dots, Toby? I heard someone say polka dots, I think it was Aunty Nettie, you remember we watched her one day through the door. She had a case with a paua shell cover, on the duchesse in front of her, and a powder puff in her hand, and was patting her face and smiling a private smile to herself in the mirror. A smile full of delight and arrangement and what is called wisdom. And then she turned and saw us and went red.

—How dare you watch me put on my face.

It was a sin. To have watched Aunty Nettie putting on her face. And it was worse for her, I suppose, because now we knew she had another face and another smile to it. We had found her out, like a thief. She kept blushing.

—You rude children.

As if we had been watching her on the lavatory or picking her nose or doing any one of those things you do in private, to yourself.

But Toby you do not get better. You do not know us or speak to us, and Chicks and I play together and wait for you to come home, and the children at school say,

—Your brother takes fits, Ya-ha.

And then when you come from hospital and walk down by the sea and they find you having a fit, the people say to our mother,

—Mrs Withers, your boy will have to be sent away.

Now Toby, I know about people being sent away and I wonder where away is. Perhaps it is down Rio where they sing a song of the fish of the sea. Away down Rio. You remember the woman up the road had to be sent away because she kept going out in the street with no clothes on, like the emperor in the story, except that people were wise, like the child, and noticed, and said,

—Hey you. You can't get away with that.

So they put her away somewhere, and also the other lady, Minnie Cuttle, who stood on top of the hill and dropped swears like hailstones on everybody in the valley, even on our mother, who would have given her food and clothing, not that she needed them but that was our mother's way of love, like giving us milk and milk to drink, and keeping a jersey cow that breathed in our face the breath of grass and cavern of milk, like love; though Chicks was too small for an extra mother, at first, and was kissed more, but not our father who said

—Get away can't you, if our mother put her arms around him or touched his shoulder.

Our father was sad, though he had a new bicycle in exchange for Francie's and had burned Francie's slacks, at last, under the copper, setting fire to them in secret, and he was guilty now and did not like to be kissed.

—Get away can't you.

And our mother would put the kettle on for a cup of tea,

and when the kettle began singing and the pot stood warm
and ready on the side of the stove, with two teaspoons of tea
in it, no, three, one for each person and one for the pot, as it
said on the outside of the packet, our mother would say with
the same look she gave our father when she wanted to kiss him,
—Have a cup of tea, Bob.
And our father, deceived, would smile,
—Just what I need. Why didn't I think of it before?
So our mother would have given the lady on the hill, Minnie
Cuttle, a hundredweight of tea in exchange for a hundredweight of swears; but they put the lady away who dropped
hailstones in the valley; and they did not put you away Toby
for our mother said, always,
—No child of mine. No child of mine.

*And so on and on. And we walk like Theseus or an ashman
in the labyrinth, with our memories unwound on threads of
silk or fire; and after slaying by what power the minotaurs of
our yesterday we return again and again to the birth of the
thread, the Where.*

*And what Theseus or ashman will wear in his hair a scarlet
poppy made of paper, or tie up his trousers like a parcel,
with string, fasten the legs of them like two Christmas
crackers with a gold thread?*

*And the sky is now a blue mask to cover memory, the ledgers,
the wonder beneath glass,*

Rapunsel, Rapunsel, let down your hair.

Drop thy pipe, thy happy pipe.

Part Two
Twenty Years After

15

TOBY

—*Sings Daphne from the dead room.*
I talk of the woodlouse and his traffic across the wall, the
turtle-turn of him and his legs writing in the air his telegram
to pity,
—*Come quick. I burrow in the closed eyes of wall and wall for*
trickle-taste of light.
sings Daphne from the dead room.
I kept a dream of two thieves under my pillow, and my thieves
are gone, full with my last meal of sleep
to a beach blessed with shell
where winter pours velvet sunlight
where small buttons like pearl
green as karaka leaf
are sewn to sleep in shrift of tide
in seabed of my brother's grief.
Listening at keyhole of summer,
I hear the roar of snow.
In case the sunlight kill
I will make you, Toby, a salt shirt
with small buttons like pearl
white as manuka bud
sewn in the sleeves that sweep the sea
all winter with your life's blood.
Looking at green wave through glass of fire
I see the red shadow.
Toby, I will give you a loaf of blue air from wheat that grows
in the sky, and trawl the wasting seas for paradisal shoal of
love, and when you die
                    sings Daphne from the dead room.
I will say you lived in a half-world, a microscopic place of
bitten oranges like blighted sunfall, where neither the

wind blowing the way forward nor the way back, articulate
with ripe fruit of night could feed or make you whole.
—Rags bones bottles scrap iron old steel a life to sell
        sings Daphne from the dead room.
Now Toby, what will you be, what will you be,
in freezing works west-coast mine or foundry?
Now Toby where will you live, where will you live
—in hovel or bungalow God forgive.
Now Toby how will you die how will you die
—dug and dumped in the pit of why.

16

Hard cash.

Toby Withers unrolled his bundle of ten shilling notes and put them down in a layered and crumpled confection of soft rust upon the table that was small and shaped like a cell of black honey.

A world ago the hives with their hats on in the corner of the
paddock and the bees in a swarm in the gorse and the
apple-blossom and the world-size apples where a child's reach
exceeds his grasp else what's a heaven for, Granny Smith,
Kentish Fillbasket, Rome Beauty, Delicious, Jonathan,
Irish Peach, and the stripey ones like eating green ice-cream,
else what's a heaven for?

Hard cash.

The ten shilling notes were from the freezing works where Toby worked in season with good money, overtime, bonus, boots provided, strip the guts all day and bring home a kidney in your pocket, a spare for your old man who's retired, sixty, sits in the corner by the stove, jigging his knee or tapping on the edge of the table with his three middle fingers, remembering the war, which war,

Fall in A

Fall in B

Fall in all the company.

The old man—

—Toby, *never* call your father the old man.

Toby's father takes pills in a narrow bottle with a red wrapper insect-ridden with instructions and warnings. Toby takes pills too for his fits that happen now only sometimes, and

54

then it is his mother, faded, shrunk, stolid, vague, with the hardened arteries and swollen belly of salt, who will comfort him. Toby is a man, thirty-two, newminted from adolescence and the twenties, a gold coin, silver coin, copper coin, ten shilling note of rust lying upon a black cell of honey.

17

It was half-past ten, the three clocks told it, for where one had stood on the mantelpiece in the Withers kitchen, fed year after year with bills and receipts and tickets, two more had been put for companionship, a gloating and clucking collection of time, a triple blackmail, the old grandfather clock and the two alarms with their moon-faces and humped shoulders. They all pointed to half-past ten, and were believed.

But the radio *knew*, and its telling, in a human voice, gave comfort to Bob and Amy and Toby Withers, sitting in the kitchen, under the spell of the thirty-six inhuman eyes.

—A quarter-past ten, the man on the radio said.

—The clocks are wrong, said Bob Withers, looking at the mantelpiece triumphantly; but even as he said The clocks are wrong, he knew they were right, and they looked down at him, idiot-shining they were, and told him they were right, and he said,

—What've we got three clocks for, anyway?

—Now, said the man on the radio—A session for bandsmen, conducted for you by Walter. Good morning, Walter.

—Turn it off, Toby said. I can't count my money while the radio's on.

He had taken a pile of silver from a tin on the mantelpiece and shaken it upon the table, and now was arranging it in columns not quite as high as the Eiffel tower.

—Turn it off.

He spoke to no one, really, but his mother appeared from the scullery, as she always appeared when he called; tied, like a gentle echo, to his talking. She held an oven cloth and her face was flushed from bending over the electric stove that stood just inside the door, in the corner,

—Oh Toby. Your grandfather belonged to the first brass band in the province. He was bandmaster. They used to parade on a Sunday. Listen. But I'll turn it off if you want it off.

—I can't count my money with the noise in my ear.

His mother obediently turned off the radio. His father looked up from by the coal range where he sat, cosy as a cricket, hopping his eyes over the morning paper. He had read the news page and the local, skimming the overseas notes about China and the Far East, and was reading up the truck accident where young Fred Maines had been injured and removed to hospital, condition fair. Then he would turn to the comic strip at the back, though he usually liked to read that first; though sometimes he tempted himself by keeping it to the last.

—Do as your mother wants you. Leave the radio on. You could have counted your money last night or any other time. Anyway you count it so often you ought to know how much you've got. Not that *I* get any of it, or your mother, for the house.

—But, Dad—

—You don't have to live here if you don't want to, if you think your mother and father are getting too old and niggely.

—Oh Bob, Toby would never think that about us, would you Toby?

—You know I wouldn't Mum. It's just that it's Dad—

—Why don't you get married? What's wrong with the Chalklin girl?

Mrs Withers looked alarmed,

—Oh Bob, you know she's just a friend. Toby's not going to get caught out marrying, are you Toby?

—Too right I'm not, Mum. And I'd like to give you some money Dad, but I've got to get going in life, and money's something to hang on to, otherwise you sink. When have *I* had a start in life? I've got commitments.

He repeated the word. Commitments. It was a long word for him because he had left school early on account of his fits, and his spelling had always been shaky, but heavens, what he had picked up in the meantime. He might stumble in speech sometimes and be slow, with his tongue lolling at the corner of his mouth, but he felt he was beginning to learn about the most important things in life, money and things like that.

—Yes, I've got commitments.

—Don't forget I've got commitments too, my boy. Rates and electric light.

—But I bought you two bags of wheat last week, for the fowls, and the canvas to make the hood for your car. Why don't you get the hood made for your car?

Mr Withers looked tired. He fingered the last page of the paper and peeped at the comic strip, Choko working in his garden and planting his cabbages upside down because he wanted to send them, without paying airmail, to his relative, his old uncle on the other side of the world. Bob thought it was not as funny as last week's where Choko gave an election speech.

—Yes, what about the hood? Toby persisted.

—I'll take my time. Don't rush me. I'm not as young as I was, remember. Nor is your mother either.

—No.

Toby looked over at his mother. She had a piece of butter-paper in her hand and was greasing the girdle for pikelets that would be made on the coal stove, the batter dropped in spoonfuls on the smoking girdle, and rising and bubbling and browning and being thrust quickly to sweat under a warm folded tablecloth. Amy Withers always made pikelets for peace. She would butter them for Bob and Toby as if the two were children, and hand them over to them on a plate, buttering and handing over, buttering and handing over till the batch was finished, or nearly, and

—Oh, I'm getting a paunch, Bob Withers would say, patting his tummy that flowed out below the two peaks of his waist-coat. He was really like a round ball, started small, but the years had wound more flesh upon him; yet one thing, he had kept his hair; it was grey and glossy and his pride

and Amy, with a pikelet in her hand,

—No wife will ever make you pikelets like these, Toby. I remember when you were little—

And she would go on to talk about the flood; not the one with the Ark and the animals two by two, and behold I even I do bring a flood of waters upon the earth to destroy all flesh wherein is the breath of life, from under heaven, and everything that is in the earth shall die; but the river flood, the Clutha churned with snow, and the stooks whirling down, and the rabbits sitting on top for comfort and convenience,

—when you were little, Toby, and Chicks wasn't born, and

you and Francie stayed at Grandma's, remember?

And fed on Amy Withers' brand of buttered olives and olive leaves, the Withers family, Toby and his mother and father, would make peace and be blessed.

And so it happened this Saturday. Toby picked up his money, stored it in the silver cocoa tin that he kept on the mantelpiece, glanced, with challenge and triumph, at his father who had taken from the other end of the mantelpiece his own silver pipe-tobacco tin where he kept the threepenny bits he saved.

Toby yawned.

—It's hot in here.

—It's the stove, Toby. Wait, I'll open a window.

—O.K. Mum, I'll shave, I think.

He went to the bedroom and plugged in his electric shaver. The sound of it, the itching whirr-whirr carried to the kitchen where Bob Withers sat, mourning now, over his handful of threepenny bits, and wishing and wishing

The Art Union? There was a theory that if you bought a ticket up north where the population was thickest you were sure to win a prize. The raffle? Tatts? He listened to the electric shaver, the new way of shaving, naked and criminal and domineering without the shaving soap and the water boiling and the bathroom door shut and the steam to be wiped off the mirror.

He thought, It's beyond me, I can't catch up.

18

Now this Saturday was the first of May, the opening of the shooting season, and the evening papers would be full of photographs of men in gumboots and waterproof jackets, leaning on rifles, and holding high the twisted neck and wet body of swan or goose or wild paradise duck that gleams blue and green like a split rainbow. And it had seemed that all night before, and early in the morning, the ducks had been flying over, low in the mist below the clouds, to find shelter in the town gardens where they mingled with their tamed and plump relatives, and with them, on the special duck pond at the gardens, were chased and stoned by children and choked with the million white-bread crumbs of their charity; or at the Withers' place where the creek flowed and pukekos took long strides through the swamp, flicking their white envelopes of tail. There on the creekside the bird refugees were free to waddle and preen, and taking the water by surprise that it had scarcely time to divide its unbroken wave to receive them, slip secretly in, flopping their calico feet, floating silently, breast-high, to the shelter of the willow, safe in shadow. There at the Withers' place they made their nest, hatched their eggs, trooped backward and forward in strict naval formation except for the littlest one, astraggle and alarmed, who spent his duckling days in the wearying effort to catch up.

—Mind the eels, his mother would say.

—Mind the eels, they swallow you whole. Come in you naughty bird.

The day promised fine, fair to fine over coastal Otago the paper said, for the paper showed every day a picture of the weather. There was someone, they said, who lived up north and sat in a tower and spent his days, not working like other people, but capturing paths of air and stringing them together to form a map of wiggles and squirls. And Bob Withers would say as he thought of the man in the tower,

—*Some* people can take it easy.

Work for him, till he retired and they gave him his travelling clock as a present but where would he ever travel so he kept the clock shut and away hidden, meant moving and sweating and carrying and hauling; not sitting in a tower, high-up and still as a week-day church bell.

So the day promised fair, and the sea lay like a quilt with the waves tucked under, and the trees wavering like leafless water, cut to fit from a transparent block of blue air and frost.

—What a day, Toby said, as he finished his shave and rubbed a bit of cream over his face. Cancer indeed, he thought. My father's afraid to move with the times. That's why he won't use an electric razor. The old lather-up and the strop and the cut-throat razor for him. Cancer or no cancer, this is *my* way. He fitted the shaver back in its leather jacket and zipped it shut. What a great day!

Great day for what, Toby?

Oh I'll go down on the flat and heap together that scrap iron for the foundry, collect the rags perhaps from Joseph's, run out to Chalklins' with the books for Jim. There's plenty to do. He

59

parted the curtains and looked down on the flat, near the creek where the ducks waddled about on the bank. A starling in the pear tree, or one of the oak trees, made a rippling sound, like silk being torn, some kind of black shiny silk or perhaps taffeta going green with age and wear.

—Duck season, Toby said. What if I get a licence to shoot? *A great day, Toby.*

—Yes, a great day with plenty to do. Pictures tonight.

Toby, it is Saturday morning a long time ago, twenty-five years, and you are busy with nothing, you spend all morning with a willow stick, breaking it from the branch, whittling it, poking it in the water, hitting the grass with it, and what do you dream, Toby?

—*I dream I go up home and find it all gone, cleaned out with a broom, and I'm going to live by the creek with Chicks an' Francie an' Daphne an' I'm goin' to eat suckers an' not have any fits, an' the sun's on us, an' I'm going to have a stick to hit with when the dark comes.*

—Yes, perhaps I will buy a rifle to shoot. Only after. But why? Or tomorrow. I don't know, I'll go around to Chalklins.

He drove his truck carefully along the main street beside the avenue of elm trees. He felt happy driving, with the needle at thirty and his foot—how would he put it?—trigger-happy upon the brake. He passed the police station at thirty. He thought, If the sergeant is there he will look from the window and see me driving and think, Toby Withers deserves to drive a car, he's more careful than those who don't take fits, it's a handicap that teaches them, what they want is a handicap. But for all the talk he's growing out of his fits they say they say.

He drove on past the unkempt and off-guard Saturday shops with their overflowing tins of rubbish like dreary signals of confession in the doorway; and the brazen milk-bar with the new class, the milk-bar cowboy, the teddy-boy, hanging around the door and putting money in the nickelodeon for

—Oh My Papa to me he was so wonderful

Oh my papa to me he was so good.

Toby hummed the rest of the song to himself as he drove. Oh my papa, retired, cut off from all that mattered to him, the railway, the all-day life-toy, oh my papa wandering down to the shed to have a look around for old time's sake, getting the gossip from the girl at the bookstall and a free cup of tea from the waitress in the refreshment rooms, just to prove how it used to be; meeting his cobbers and talking their private language of the biscuit,

She's got too much of a grade

Oamaru Timaru Waianakarua,

He Hi the blowfly.

And then seeing the new cleaners and firemen and drivers, the bits of kids trying to manage things and getting paid handsomely for it too

—not like in my day, why when I was starting we were lucky to earn—

money money, the same old story, but *oh my papa*.

Toby turned the corner to where the Chalklins lived. Marry Fay Chalklin? Marry her and be a husband like the rest of the chaps around thirty, with a house built in the right style and the right things put inside it, the sort of things a girl would like, the new furniture that you can't sit on, the chairs with legs like an operating table, and the skinny mantelpiece that sits above a fraud fire. Marry Fay Chalklin and be in with people again, or when was it ever any time, and not go to the pictures of a Saturday night alone, sitting in the middle back stalls and reading the Saturday night sports paper in the interval, trying to find some place to be, even if it's in a paper scrum or a printed wrestling match; or going out for a smoke alone, standing by the corner near the torn hoardings with the faded and stained pictures of a show or circus that came and stayed two nights and went on to the end of the world with its fat lady and little man two feet high and king lion asking out of its filth and straw

—How much land does a king require?

Marry Fay Chalklin and squat on a quarter acre section, a government house perhaps, that exists in spawns or litters, alike of the same mother and father the government architect. In a suburb of revolving clotheslines and a free kindergarten. With people people and no place alone, and what did my mother read, twenty-five years ago from the Bible,

Woe unto them that join house to house, that lay field to field till there be no place that they may be placed alone in the midst of the earth.

Toby closed his eyes and opened them again, quickly, in case the world changed suddenly and there were some corner to hide in, belonging. Oh marry Fay Chalklin and not ever be on the outside of the circle that whirled round and round faster than any light and letting no part break for a man to squeeze in and be warm, my God, an epileptic too.

Toby Withers, the shingle-short with the dirty fingernails and the brown greasy hair and the heavy shoulders and the head on one side and the thick neck with valleys of flesh at the hairline. With the room at home, off the kitchen, next to Mum and Dad. Grey blankets on the bed, single bed, socks from yesterday stuffed, smelling, at the bottom under the bedclothes, chamber in the middle of the floor, full of cigarette butts floating like white dead torpedoes wrecked on the amber seas of night. And the pills, the pills in the narrow tall packet, one to be taken in the morning and one at night, T. Withers. For fits.

Fits. Fits. Fits. He falls down anywhere you know. They say he can tell when they come on, it's a wonder they have given him a licence to drive, he had a struggle to get his present licence, in court and all, with his own doctor saying,

—Withers is no danger

they say they say

how he is better than he used to be, remember, when they would find him any place, on the road or the beach, not being drowned, the waves gentle upon him, washing his heart out with salt,

they say they say

they're a queer family though, you remember his sister Francie was burned in that fire and his other sister Daphne got stranger and stranger, the one that went on to High School, learning things and reading, and they put her away in a hospital, an asylum

they say

and his other sister, Chicks, they used to call her, that's Teresa, married early, it was a have-to marriage to some student when she was nursing, and they went up north

they say they say

it's the sort of thing that runs in families, it's just as well he isn't married, but his heart's kind, remember he helped that old man and gave him somewhere to live, and bedding and food; but he's mean with money, he's married to money, pennies and threepences and sixpences, and pound notes wrapped around him like an overcoat to keep him warm from the outside cold; he'd give everything away but his money

they say they say
and he reads. Sometimes he reads queer things
and didn't he drink once but it was hushed up
didn't he travel round the world in a sailing vessel or was it
round and round himself?

The Chalklins were not at home, neither Jim nor Mrs, nor
Fay. The blinds were down and an empty milk bottle, patched
inside with dust, stood in the box by the gate.

—They must be home, Toby thought. It's Saturday morning
 and they're never out on a Saturday morning.

He went around to the back door and knocked loudly,
hearing no movement inside but silence. The chimney had no
smoke and the washhouse door was wedged shut with a piece
of newspaper. There was a tea-towel hanging on one peg from
the clothesline.

A neighbour looked over the fence and saw Toby.

—They're away for the weekend, she said, glad to possess
 information and glad to part with it—What a great day,
 isn't it?

She smiled at him.

—You're Toby Withers, aren't you? I *thought* you looked
 like Toby Withers. The family's away for the weekend,
 Mrs and Mr and Fay, though Fay's gone to the Crudge's,
 Albert's her fiance you know. Fancy getting married. It'll
 be a change from working in the woollen mill all week
 and every week till she's tired out.

—Will it? Toby said.

—Yes, you know how pale they get, being inside all day.

—And getting married, said Toby, she will live outside then?

The neighbour looked surprised—How funny of you to say
that. She'll live in a house.

—Oh, said Toby.

—And now, said the neighbour, I must fly. Give my regards
 to your mother, and now I really must fly.

—My husband's away in the swamp, shooting for ducks, she
 said.

And Toby said, *But I came for Fay to take her with me, for
her to be my wife and myself to be her husband. I thought we
should go down on the beach in the lupins, but sit for a while
first and watch the sea coming in and the dark blue waves
curled over like the beak of a bird spitting lace, yes I came for
Fay, I was going to pull her hair off and float it on the sea like*

63

weed and take my rifle shining and new with oil and shoot my
little paradise duck and pick the drab tired feathers from her
body
 and bandage with love the scar upon her neck
 her neck that I will twist for her to die
 the scar that leather has made, the leather strap of the mill
 girl day after day, oh yes I came for my wife.
—Are you all right, Toby? the neighbour asked.

Toby frowned at her.

—I thought you were gone, he said, to the swamp, to be shot.

The neighbour looked alarmed and hurried away inside to tell someone about queer Toby Withers but there was no one to tell and say *Just imagine* to; which is the worst of living, having no one around at the time to tell.

Toby drove home, slowly. He felt tired. Pictures tonight, he thought. Oh hell. But I mustn't swear because my mother disapproves. Poor mum, I'll stand by her.

He parked his truck on the flat and crossed the bridge to the house. The wild ducks, the refugees, sat on the water like decoys. Toby's footsteps startled them to a tremble of green and blue feather across the brown taut sheet of water that tucked itself into the banks of the creek, amongst the mint growing tall and the sleeping bulbs of narcissus and jonquil.

—Duck duck duck Toby called, clicking his tongue and feeling in his pocket for crumbs, but what would crumbs be doing in his pocket, never mind, duck duck duck you little beauties.

 Dreamed I saw a building with a thousand floors
 a thousand windows and a thousand doors
 not one of them was ours, my dear,
 not one of them was ours.

He went up the path to the house. It was near lunch time and he could smell the stew with its sunken rocks of potatoes eddied and swum with gravy and shreds of steak clinging together in their drowned and warm world. His mother opened the door,

—Oh Toby, she said. As if he had been away travelling for a hundred or thousand years and had only just returned. She seemed to search him, his heavy weather-beaten face for sign of salt storm from an unknown ocean, his large oil-stained hands for what he might bring in them for her—ivory, peacocks, violets, gold—

—ah gold.

And she greeted him with her old love-invitation to food, as if he had starved on his voyaging.

—Oh Toby, you'll want something to eat. Come and have your lunch. Did you see the Chalklins?

She said the Chalklins, but she did not mean them, she meant the worlds of people on other islands beyond the Withers island with its huddled Bob and Amy and Toby and its wild ducks crying out, this morning, beneath the winter clouds.

—Did you see the Chalklins?

—They were out.

—Oh, that's funny, they're never out in the weekend. Was Fay home perhaps?

—No, she was away too.

—Well I'll get your lunch dished up and call your father, said Amy, in a tone of triumph, like a happy magician about to perform an infallible sleight of hand and heart.

—But, your father's up the back, he's been there for half an hour. I tell him to go to the doctor but he just keeps taking those pills.

She leaned to Toby and whispered

—He bleeds.

—He's a fool not to see about it then.

—Oh, don't go quarrelling with him, Toby. You know what your father is. Listen, there are the ducks calling out. But they know they're safe at our place. They have somewhere to go.

—Yes, said Toby, they have somewhere to go.

19

Have you ever been to the pictures in the town where the Withers live? There are two theatres opposite each other, the Regent and the Miami. At the Regent the prices are higher and the films what are called first-class without any intrusion of moronic cartoon or ride-'em-cowboy serials or half-naked women stranded in rubber plantations and beset upon by perspiring white men in topees and shorts, the acknowledged tropical dress. The toffs, the rich and educated, go to the Regent in their best clothes and furs. There is a fake night sky in the ceiling, covered with stars that are fixed to twinkle realistically in the central-heated air, above the rows of looking and rustling and hushing rich and prosperous people. The lights go out, the stars fade, there is a murmur of pleasure. Oh what luxury even to breathe.

The Miami, especially in winter, is austere and cold with an icy wind blowing through the heavy velvet curtains at the back. The unenlightened people go there, to whistle and sing out and rustle chocolate papers and blow through their teeth Whe-e-e-e whenever the hero and heroine kiss, or when she throws her clothes from behind a curtain and you know she is either going to bed or about to have a censored bath. The crowd like the kissing and the touching and the fights with pulled hair and slapped faces.

—You brute, how dare you.

—My darling, you are everything in the world to me.

The Miami, because of its lower caste, does not cost as much as the Regent. If you want to look at the stars there, you go outside to see them fretting their light with frost and cold cloud. They cannot be extinguished with a turn of a switch and you do not pay for them.

If you had been at the Miami theatre on the night of the first of May you would have seen Toby Withers sitting by himself in the fourth from the back row. He wore his new tie and his dark blue suit, his best. His shoes were polished and his rough brown hair glistened with hair-cream that he bought in a heart-shaped bottle and kept on the shelf in the bathroom. His hands were red and engrained with dirt and hung ashamed and awkward with no hiding-place. In his pocket, though you could not see them, he was keeping them for when the picture started, there was a sixpenny roll of fruit-flavoured sweets, some orange and raspberry, lemon, strawberry, Toby could not tell which until he opened them, it was always a surprise. Also he had a bar of chocolate. And in his other pocket a copy of the Saturday night Sports Special, a sick yellow colour, where the racing news was printed, and results of football and shield games; a page of problem letters to Uncle Jamie, a comic strip of travel on the moon, and an article on the Real Inside Life of Hollywood. Toby was keeping the Sports paper till after, when he went home, and then he would draw it from his pocket, and his father, going to bed, would stop in the kitchen doorway,

—Let us look at the sports, he would say, extending his hand.

And Toby would spread it out upon the table,

—I haven't read it myself, he would say, powerfully holding tight to the sick yellow treasure, not wanting to read it but crying and laughing inside himself at the way his father cringed in the doorway for a drug-drop of the sick magic.

So he sat by himself in the pictures. One time an usher showed a young woman to the seat next to Toby, and he reached to turn it down for her and smiled at her. But her boyfriend was following and he sat down and they drew close and whispered and giggled and ate wine gums, poking their tongues out to see what colour they were

—Mine's what colour?

—Green, what's mine?

—Yours is green too.

—They must have both been lemon.

And they thought this astounding deduction very funny and laughed and laughed that they had eaten a lemon sweet.

Toby thought, If they carry on this way, I shan't be able to hear the picture, it's just like them to sit next to me and behave like schoolchildren. Ah, it's beginning now. Why did I come? Why do I ever do anything? When will I stop taking fits? There's Mrs Crat and her husband, how old she looks; and he too, I remember when they seemed quite young and she used to stand at her washhouse door and laugh, and no one knew why she laughed, standing there at her washhouse door and looking outside at the world. She used to carry messages home on a Friday, her arm almost bending to touch the ground with the weight of the basket. We borrowed their spade and never gave it back. And there's Bill Trout and Mary. How funny. We tin-canned them and threw rice at them and they gave us a cream bun that was only half cream. And now he's one of the heads at the freezing works, with his face like a hunk of meat, and fat, and when he went for his holiday to the city only last week and one of the chaps saw him there, and I said to the chap What was he doing when you saw him he answered,

—Why, looking in the window of a butcher's shop.

They've one little girl who lies down and screams and is spoilt, they say. It seems as if everyone's here tonight that I know, all crowding in. Some day I will get out of this and go up north perhaps or somewhere to a new place and set up business and be comfortable and rich and loved; but it's too late.

He unrolled the top sweet of the packet and popped it in his mouth. It was a raspberry sweet. He thought, my tongue will be red now. Is it? But I cannot ask anyone to find out. I think the next sweet will be orange, or it may be another raspberry, sometimes there are two raspberries, one after the other, or lemon, or cherry, it is exciting to guess.

He crumpled the silver paper tight, pounding it close with his fist. His hand shook slightly, and he dropped the paper on the floor. And the cartoon began. He stared at the screen and watched the tiny man growing bigger and bigger and slaying a wild lion.

The audience relaxed and laughed, warm and satisfied.

20

Toby did not write letters. He was surprised to receive one the following week from Fay Chalklin, who said in neat handwriting, Dear Toby, I was away last week and did not see you but our neighbour said you called with the books for Dad. On Sunday (this next Sunday) Dad is having a birthday tea and would like you to come if you can. Dad has asked me to write this letter for him, as he is hopeless at letters. Yours sincerely Fay Chalklin.

Amy Withers brought the letter up from the box at the gate. She was breathless and holding her hand over her heart and in her hand was the letter. She put it on the mantelpiece, face up, so Toby would see it when he came home, and she sat down on the sofa. Her face was flushed and she felt tired. It's my heart, she thought, that makes me this way. It'll give out one of these days or nights. I wonder who the letter's from. I'll just lie here and watch the wax-eyes on top of the old dunny roof, and then I'll see about making the shortbread for the weekend.

Toby came home tired and cold and with the local paper in his hand. He sat down to read it first before his father came in from the garden.

—Any mail?

—A letter for you, Toby. The mail was late.

—It's always late these days. Why don't you ring up about it?

—I will, Toby, if it comes late again.

—But you always say you will and you never do.

—Why don't you read your letter? It's probably from your girlfriend, said Amy softly and insinuatingly.

Toby blushed. —Go on, Mum, you know who *my* girlfriend is. He looked at her and smiled. —You look hot, Mum. Sit down and have a rest. She laughed. —Take off those heavy gumboots, Toby, and get your feet warm. I'll call your father for a cup of tea. He's out in the garden. The beans have escaped the frost.

—Have they? It's from Fay Chalklin, Mum. She wants me to go around on Sunday night for a birthday tea. I'll have to see whether I'll be busy or not.

Amy Withers looked afraid. Toby was her only son, and when his fits came, who was it who looked after him and told him to have faith? And ironed his shirts and darned his socks?

Toby opened the evening paper.

—By the way, Mum, I've got a contract for pulling down the Peterkin Hotel, so I've given up at the Freezing Works. It'll mean money.

—Will you go to the party, Toby?

—Oh it's not a party, Mum, just a high tea.

Bob Withers came in the door, glanced suspiciously at Toby and Amy, then sat down in his favourite chair by the fire.

—I've beat the frost, Mum, he said.

—Oh Bob, I'm so glad. And are the potatoes in?

—Yes, potatoes and peas and cabbage.

—Oh Bob, isn't that lovely.

She looked proudly at her husband who had beaten the frost, and then proudly at her son who was going to pull down a hotel, and earn more and more money; but afraid of him she felt, because of the more and more money, and the party, the invitation for next Sunday.

And she stood there handing out tea. She was getting withered and old but what would Bob and Toby have done without her, she was like an old worn letter-box standing there year after year and having posted in her all the bits of news and worry and fear and love that came from her husband and son. And then she would jiggle the news inside her, to pass it from one to the other and establish peace between them. So

—Oh Bob, Toby's got a special invitation from Fay Chalklin to go there for her birthday on Sunday.

She spoke calmly, torturing herself with the meaning of the words.

—Got you in her clutches at last, has she Toby?

Toby remained silent. He rustled the newspaper, to revenge himself and make his father realize that here was the evening paper and Toby was first to read it. Bob Withers leaned forward,

—Give us the outside page, Toby, he said.

Toby got up from the sofa. —You can have the lot, Dad, I'm finished with it. It's full of nothing. And Fay Chalklin, by the way is engaged to be married.

—You're teasing, said his mother delightedly.

Toby looked at her as if to say, Yes, I'm teasing, it's not true; then he gave a mysterious smile and went to his room and sat down upon the bed. He withdrew the letter from his pocket and read it. He thought, Yours sincerely Fay Chalklin. Putting her surname too, and saying, Mum and Dad would like you to come Mum and Dad would like you to come. If I tear off the bottom bit and leave the letter lying around, no one will know that she did not say Yours passionately, Fay. Or Very much love. But who would find it and where would I leave it lying around? And who would care if they found it, or wonder what it said. Love from Fay. But if only. He read the letter aloud, every word of it, from the beginning, Dearest Toby, to the end, Yours passionately, and he smiled as he read it. Then he smelt the letter. Lavender, lily of the valley, French Fern, what were the scents his sisters had used? Chicks who was up north and married with children, in a posh house with all the latest gadgets, and Francie who was burned young, and he had sat on the sofa in the Harlow's house, that was Chick's mother-in-law's place now, and taken a fit because a giant hedgehog squeezed through the door after him, its quills on fire; and Daphne, in hospital and strange for a long time now.

Yours passionately, Fay.

> *Dreamed I saw a building with a thousand floors*
> *a thousand windows and a thousand doors*
> *Not one of them was ours, my dear.*
> *Not one of them was ours.*

He had read that somewhere, why did he remember it?

Then he tore up the letter and took his purse from his

pocket to count his money, for money was the chief treasure now; and he rubbed his thumb around the serrated edges of the sixpences and shillings and florins and halfcrowns. He rolled the silver and coppers along the dressing-table until they lost balance and fell still. By next year, he thought, I should have enough money to set up a real business of my own. Or earlier. And sit back and relax.

21

Toby did not go to the birthday party. Nor did he go, in the spring time to Fay Chalklin's wedding to Albert Crudge, though he read about it in the paper and he received an invitation done in curly silver writing.

—You will send a present, though Toby, his mother said.

—What can I send her?

His mother said, —Well, not something personal, like underclothes or jewellery; just something small, perhaps for the household, the kitchen or dining room, or something to put flowers in, anything small and useful. That's how it was done in my day.

So Toby bought a pair of best linen sheets and half a dozen tea-towels and took them round one afternoon a week before the wedding. Fay was at home by herself and she asked him past the front room where the presents were lying on the table and upon the settee.

—Thank you so much for the useful present, Toby. Everybody has been so good to me.

She sounded surprised.

—You've no idea how kind everybody is. The old lady along the road has sent me the dearest linen teashower, done in blue in the corners, willow pattern, with the lovers crossing the bridge and those lovely wavy Chinese trees. I would so much like to go to China. Wouldn't it be wonderful if Albert and I ended up in China?

—Yes, Toby said, thinking, She worked at the Woollen Mills. I wonder if she is blind and if her eyes have changed to neon bulbs. Her face is pale. Her hands move backwards and forwards like shuttles filled with dream of her tomorrow when she will die.

—China is my favourite country, Fay said. I've always liked China.

She spoke of it as if it were a food that had been offered her since childhood, and that she had eaten and relished while others refused it as unpalatable.

—I like India, Toby said.

—Do you, Toby? How curious. Come and sit down while I make a cup of tea. You know Albert of course?

Toby said Yes, that he knew Albert. He did not say that Albert Crudge was the little boy who used to wait at the school gates and pitch into Toby every afternoon, and Toby could never hit him back because Albert had been a cripple then, and walked with a stick.

—Ya, fits, fits, fits, Albert used to say.

But he was only a boy then. Now he was a man working in the Social Security Department, helping people to fill in forms and decide how much money they earned; stamping envelopes and sending out benefits for sickness; interviewing people in confidence. His was a high-up job now, and though he was still partly a cripple he drove through the town in a modern green car that crouched low on the ground and had venetian blinds in the back.

He is one of the men who wrote in the ledgers, perhaps, thought Toby. And Fay is one of the girls who rode their bicycles, how did Daphne and Francie say it,

into the north wind, or chased by the south wind that brought snow the white parcel, unravelled and scattered.

And now the two marry, the imprisoned man and the white as milk woman, and they will die. They are my own age but they have lived since I was a little boy, and then they were the same age as they are now, for they have stopped, have been wedged in a dark since I was a small boy and watched them, with Francie and Daphne and Chicks, who was youngest and had to catch up and have stones or sand emptied out of her shoe. Or they are different bodies but the same people.

Fay went from the room to put the kettle on for a cup of tea. She was singing,

Seven lonely days make one lonely week
la-di-la-la-la-la-la-di-da.

Ever since the day that you came along.

She's happy, thought Toby. She has long hair like all the

mill girls when the fashion is that way, done with a kind of bob thing at the back, some say it is false hair, that you may buy in the hairdressers where plaster heads of women sit in the window with their gold and dark permed hair and the place is filled with the smell of burning as you pass the door. Perhaps, he thought, Fay wears false hair, and she will take it off at night and hang it on a nail in the corner of her bedroom. And Albert will not mind, for he wears a false heart; his other heart was eaten out by corrosive ink and typewritten upon like a form to be filled in.

And Fay, Toby thought, wears lipstick, to pretend there is blood in her pallor, that all her blood has not been drawn, year after year, into the neon sunlight of the mill that draws blood as the natural sunlight draws flowers. She ties her lips with red ribbon, in a bow, that Albert Crudge will undo, and both will find their empty strongbox of heart, and not know that the Social Security Department and the Woollen Mills have the key and will not part with it, ever. And if I had really loved Fay, and she loved me, and we married, I should have paid instalments of myself to the factory till I became bankrupt and a whirling spiritless machine that makes the same speech day after day till its life ends.

Toby looked at Fay as she entered the room and wondered if the brand of the mill girl was still on her shoulder where she had been whipped and led with the factory strap.

Was the mark of it there, as it had been that afternoon when she went with him to the beach and he threw her hair upon the water and shot her heart and plucked her bird-feathers?

Fay set the tea down beside him on the table.

—Don't stare at me, Toby. I'm practising for when I'm a real hostess. Do you have milk and sugar? Weak or strong?

—Milk and sugar, Toby answered promptly. Please.

She regarded him, smiling and thinking, He certainly knows what he wants. They say his mother looks after him too well. I hope Albert remembers to treat me as his wife and not as his mother to be fetching and carrying for him.

As she poured Toby's cup of tea she thought with excitement, Albert has strong tea with no milk. I shall remember that all my life. And he takes *two* teaspoons of sugar.

—Have a cake, Toby. I made them.

Toby listened while Fay gave the recipe for the cakes she

had made.

—And you must weigh everything very carefully when you are cooking particularly the flour, and never let the baking powder get moist. Now don't think I'm getting all domesticated just because I'm getting married. Don't think it because it's true.

She smiled at him once more. She felt sorry for Toby Withers, shingle short that he seemed to be, with his goofy look and his fits and his obsession with money, though *that* wasn't anything to be sorry for, in fact admired. Albert had it. Oh Oh, she thought, I have got the right husband, I know. And the house will have the new type of venetian blind that you don't have to dust, the latest of latest blinds. Poor Toby. He's never had a girl that I know of.

—No, I never liked cooking before, Toby, but I do now, she said proudly.

—Do you like them?

Toby said he liked their flavour. He felt tired of being in the room; he believed he had been having a kind of fit, but could not be sure. But he wanted to leave Fay and go home and count his money to make sure of it all. He wanted to go home and take out the new Atlas he had bought, and read it through and through, the places with their names and the beautiful colours of the pastureland and cornlands and the pictures of the mountains with their tiny threepenny caps of snow. He wanted to sit alone in his room and trace his finger over the lands of the world. And read in the diagrams about gold and iron and steel, and see the compressed bundles of wheat and the various blue seas, his own Tasman and Pacific, and oceans further off and bluer, Indian, Antarctic, Adriatic.

But Fay said, —You must see my presents Toby.

And she led him to the front room that seemed full of blankets and sheets and towels and pots and pans and knives and forks and cups and saucers and clocks,

—And this is my dinner service from the Mortons. And this is the teashower. Isn't it lovely? I'm showing you all these because you say you are not coming to the wedding. I'm really having an evening to show off my presents. And look at all the handkerchiefs and salad servers.

She was overwhelmed and excited.

—And the girls at work gave me a pop-up toaster and toast racks, I had a presentation, and the manager gave a speech and said what a good worker I had always been. I don't know, when you are getting married people treat you different all together. I used to get told off for lazing and then they say I was a good worker and they were sorry to lose me.

—What was it like working at the Mill?

—Oh, the same as anywhere, I suppose. Machines and noise, but morning and afternoon tea sharp. And ten per cent reduction, or more, on the woollen goods. I got the blankets for my box almost as soon as I started at the mill.

—And will you sleep in them, in your new house, and they won't remind you?

—Don't be silly, Toby. It's not the blankets I'll think of when I go to sleep.

Toby looked embarrassed. Then he asked seriously,

—Did you wear a leather strap?

—A what?

—A leather strap. Around your neck so that it made a mark. They used to say—

Fay interrupted, —Oh, that was an old story, surely you didn't believe *that*. It was a *child's* story, and not true.

—But child's stories are always true.

—Giants and fairies as well? Toby Withers!

—Yes, giants and fairies, in different shapes. There's a giant bomber and a giant loneliness.

Fay looked sympathetically at Toby. Poor man. To think he was thirty years old or over thirty. And believed about the strap and its mark.

Fay put on a mischievous air, —You can look if you like, about the strap, she said. Would you like to look and make sure?

—Don't be silly. I just wondered.

—I dare you to look.

Fay was enjoying herself. She pulled down her jersey to reveal her shoulder and part of her breast. She wore a pink flimsy thing underneath, with lace. Toby could see through it. He stared horrified and fascinated while Fay smiled at him enticingly

—Toby Withers, haven't you seen a bare shoulder in your life before? Don't look so scared.

—I'm not scared, said Toby, blushing, and the more he thought of himself as not scared, the more he blushed.

I think, Fay Chalklin, that you're a common woman to half undress in front of me when you're nearly married.

—I'm sorry Toby, but you're so *raw*. But thank you for the lovely presents and I'm sorry you can't come to the wedding. Goodbye Toby, and I'm sorry I haven't the mark on my shoulder.

Toby turned as he went out side the door, —But you *have* got the mark, Fay. I saw it there. We all carry some kind of mark like that because we are all branded in our lives, as I was. That is true. I don't know much, not how to spell anyway, I shall never learn to spell and what to say to people like you, but I've got books in my room, atlases that tell about the world and the seas and the first map of everywhere.

And he did not say goodbye but hurried down the path to his truck. He climbed in and drove away while Fay watched through the window. She was thinking, I'm frightened. In spite of the teashower done in blue and the plates and sheets and the silver apostle teaspoons. I'm frightened, because there's something going to happen, and Toby Withers is so strange he makes me feel the mill has captured me and wound me up like a mummy. And she buttoned up her jersey and put her hand across her shoulder where the mark of the leather strap was said to be; and then she burst into tears, and when her mother came home she found her there with all her presents and crying, and said,

—It's wedding nerves, Fay. Not long now and you'll be in that little home of your own, sweeping the doorstep and hanging out your washing on the new clothes-line.

And so it happened. Fay was married, a spring bride, and looking the social page of the newspaper said—radiant in white nylon over lace with an heirloom veil held in place by a tiny sprig of orange blossom.

And Albert's cousin Gloria, who was in the church choir, sang The Lord is my Shepherd, I shall not want. And after the wedding there was a breakfast, really a supper because it was an evening wedding, but they called it a breakfast, in the Brown's Hall, which was twice as expensive to hire as the Cosy Nook restaurant; and there were three kinds of cream cakes, and plenty of fruit salad, no liquor of course, only soft drinks because the Chalklins and Crudges, the parents, did not approve; but returns of everything if you asked for them, even though the waitresses were working late, and tired out and crochety. Oh it was a beautiful wedding, everybody said so, and the bride and bridegroom went away late that very night to the Lakes for their honeymoon.

And that night Toby sat in his room reading his Atlas. In the inside cover was a map written in old writing which said

A New Map of the Terraceous Globe according to The Ancient Discoveries and First General Divisions of it into Continents and Oceans.

Toby read the words over and over and then he turned the pages to the South and North Poles and the rest of the world that was not ice, all in pale colour of seashells. Gulf of Guinea. Morocco. Asia. He touched the gold piles of wheat and the swamp grass and the monsoon forests and the salt flats, plantless rock deserts and the terrible tiny mass of black that meant a million people crouched on a world of yellow sunlight. And he crossed the seas, Tasman, Pacific, Adriatic, Antarctic, and the continent, unnamed, on the last page, that was burned through with the mark of a leather storm; he crossed the seas with one stroke of his dirty red hand. How simple to travel, and on a night like this too, a spring night with the air outside so thick with hawthorn and plum and powdered catkin that it had to be elbowed and brushed aside before it could be breathed.

The willows down on the banks of the creek were showing their tenderest green, and the pear trees too, and the oaks, mother-wide, by the old pig sty, and wondering with every sprout of infant leaf, Who will eat our acorns when they grow? Years ago the people before the Withers had kept pigs that used to snuffle among the dead oak leaves and swallow the coffin-polished acorns that rained down, like death, and were trodden in the earth and squashed, until some shot up like little green periscopes, and

—Little by little,

Amy Withers would say, who remembered and liked to quote verse,

—Little by little the acorn said.

If you looked outside on this spring night you would think there would never be any winter or blot of death, only tonight and tonight, and people getting married and having their photos taken to put in the paper or keep on their mantelpiece for the first ten years, and then put away in the drawer; and having rice thrown at them, and the keys of their suitcase stolen for fun; and for ever after, perplexed young-old men of thirty-two sitting alone in their bedroom and travelling across blue-bag seas to fields of paper corn; only tonight and tonight and mothers and fathers sitting in their kitchen, half asleep, half listening to the radio talking to them of soap and floor-polish and Ceylon tea; and then drinking their own cups of tea and eating shortbread with the holes pricked for it to breathe; and all the Chicks living up north, far away and grown-up, but writing down from beside their spaceheaters that breathed a dragon-warmth, —We are coming south to live. Tim has bought a house there. Excuse the letter-card.

And all the Daphnes sitting somewhere in a mad hospital, in a small room with a shut window and a bed of straw and singing; and all the Francies being burned for ever in a toi-toi hollow of mind.

You would think this night that the world sated with blossom and love and death would finish and there would be no memory of it anywhere, save perhaps on a cave wall of new time, where the posturing figures dance unseen their stillness of clay or chalk or stone.

You would think all this on a spring night.

Except the thinking is not real.

22

A week later Toby received through the post a small silver tin of wedding cake from Mr and Mrs Albert Crudge. It was in a nest made of pink and blue threads of coloured paper. He was about to eat it, or at least taste it, when his mother said,

—Toby, Toby, you sleep with it under your pillow and you dream of the person you will marry. No, no—she corrected. That's only for a girl. If *you* sleep with it under your pillow you will dream of your future, and it brings good luck. Not that I believe in good luck, it is all the Lord's will. It's just a quaint superstition of putting the cake under your pillow.

Toby said he was sure he would not sleep with cake under his pillow.

And his mother said, —Well, we'll send it to Daphne, then, poor soul, I wonder how she is. They never seem to tell us, and she never seems to write and we can't visit her. I'm sure she would like a piece of wedding cake.

So it was arranged to send the cake to Daphne, and Toby put it on his dressing-table to remember to post it the next day. But that night as he got into bed he thought, well, I've seen Dad asleep with cake under his pillow; cake, wedding and Christmas, as well as those Cornish elves he sends for, dipped in magic water, that will grant every wish. It might bring me luck. I need luck to pull down the Peterkin Hotel and make money. It's a silly superstition but there's no harm in trying.

He put the tin under his pillow and turned over to sleep. He thought first of Fay Chalklin—no, Fay Crudge, and her husband, with factories and ledgers locked in them, and he wondered what Fay was doing at this time, and how she liked being married, and whether she would look any different when he saw her next time. Would she be having a baby? What would it be like to have a son or daughter? And a wife, having a wife, what would that be like?

And then Toby thought of the world, of Barcelona and Berlin and London, and some words that kept in his mind,

—*Say this city has ten million souls.*

And he thought of the short grass, tall grass, bunch grass, mountain grassland, swamp grass, mangroves. Of desert savanna and salt flats. Of pack ice and mean annual precipitation. Of all continents, scarred and burned by wind and rain. And his nose was itchy, and he picked a little ball out of it and rolled it round between his thumb and forefinger, and wiped it on his pillow. Then he curled himself up warm as an embryo and went to sleep, floating without breath on an Adriatic sea, a Gulf Stream of grey water.

And he dreamed.

And in his dream he sat in a cold apple orchard on a corner of the moon. He sat in a circle of toi-toi that hung with apples of ice. He would have picked one and eaten it, for he liked apples, but three witches danced about him, singing the same words that Daphne had told him they sang, three witches, on the heath with Hecate, in thunder and lightning.

—He shall live a man forbid, they sang.

Then they stopped singing and sat down, cross-legged, with their long skirts over their knees, and they rocked three cradles that were made, each one, of a corner of the moon; and Toby wondered where the fourth corner lay, and he felt afraid until he remembered he was sitting on it in an ice-cold apple orchard. But where is the world, he thought? I need a tiny telescope, even a toy one made of a stick of toffee that I could eat afterwards, only I need a telescope, a toy one cheap and plastic from Woolworths, yet stronger for my needs than the walking stick of Albert Crudge; and I will not spend much money on my telescope; only to look that I may know the world and see my life and my mother and father and three sisters on their island with the fire at the centre and the sea with its green web of forgetting; and across it, Fay Chalklin, the mill girl, and her Albert, the Social Security man, inhabiting where I shall never sail; and he has taken his wife, I know he has taken her, and sliced her in pale coloured slices like a seashell to be thrown back, day by day to the water; and pressed her like a flower between the pages of a large black book of judgment that has written on the outside, in frilly silver writing like a wedding invitation,

> A New Map of the Terraceous Globe according to the
> Ancient Discoveries and First General Divisions of it
> into Continents and Oceans.

Then in his dream Toby began to cry because he was alone and took fits and the middle witch left off rocking the cradle and came up to him, and said,

—Don't cry, Toby, have an apple. We are safe here. No one will know it has been stolen.

She gave him an apple of ice that melted green and red in his warm hand, the green changing to sea, the red into blood, and both flowing in salt streams across the corner of the moon. He washed his face and hands in the two streams, trying to take the black away from under his fingernails, and the nicotine from his fingers; while the three witches that were called Francie, Daphne and Chicks, rocked the cradles that held themselves as children, dreaming, with sticky warm faces, like kittens set down to suckle furry mother sleep.

—But where am I, thought Toby. There is no place for me. Where is my cradle?

—Why don't you rock me, he asked the three witches.

And one or all of them answered,

—We are afraid of you, Toby. You will take a fit.

And then he wondered again, Where is the world? He thought, perhaps I should ask the witches where the world can be, for I need money and food and clothing and some kind of social position. I shall be arrested here as a tramp and thrown in the sea or burned when morning comes and the old fires are relit in the circle of toi-toi.

He beckoned to Francie.

—Francie, you are the eldest and can tell me. Where can I find some money to have for treasure?

Francie laughed and shook her long skirt. He saw that her eyebrows had been plucked and she wore lipstick.

—Toby, don't you know this is our treasure place right here, *you know*, the books and valuable writings and things that we find, and we sit here, and the sky rolls round and round like a blue and white and grey milky marble. Oh Toby, don't you know? And the pine tree with the needles that fall and sew up our crying. She twirled her skirt again and frowned like a real witch and said, in a superior way, Don't believe me, then, if you don't want to. But ask Daphne or Chicks. Go on, ask them. Or I'll tell.

—Who will you tell?

—I'll tell Dad and then you'll be given a hiding, and have to fill the coal-bucket while he watches and gives orders. Or I'll tell mum, but she won't do anything to hurt you. She'll warn you and kiss you.

—Or I'll tell God, and *then* you'll be sorry. He'll write in his book about you, and on resurrection day, in all the crowd, with the people looking and everything, God'll read out your name from the platform and you'll have to go up in front of him and be judged, while we watch you, while everybody watches. And it'll be hot in the crowd, with so many people, and they'll be selling ice creams and cold drinks as fast as they can make them, but *you* won't get any ice creams or cold drinks, fizzy and coloured, or candy-floss either. Or be able to go and see the bearded lady and fat man when it's interval, and God has tea in the special tent. Yes, Toby Withers, I'll tell on you.

—What'll you tell about?

—I've forgotten now, but I'll tell, you see.

And Francie twirled her skirt again and began to rock the

cradle, singing, as she rocked,

—Come in you naughty bird, the rain is pouring down.

And Toby turned to Chicks and said,

—Chicks, I shall spend my life in prison if I have no money. Where can I find some money?

Chicks stopped rocking her cradle and came forward to him, and put her arm around his shoulder. Then she withdrew it quickly,

—Toby, your neck is greasy, and your hair, too, with that oil, if you are not careful you will get boils on the back of your neck and they will take a long time to heal. You will have to have penicillin, and that may shorten the time. One of the children had boils only last year and I had such difficulty. The doctor said he had never seen a case quite like it in children. It was unique, he said. He had to give the children some kind of special treatment, some drug newer than penicillin, very expensive; but of course we have the money to pay, Tim earning what he does. But the price of things these days is fantastic. You say you want money. You will never find it here. What we used to think of as treasure wasn't really treasure at all. Ours was a childish outlook, not allowable in an adult who has to adjust himself to a complex society. I'm trying to bring my children up to fit in with things. When in Rome, I say. I am training them to handle money, for money is the most important thing, or almost, in this society. I am glad you realise that money is the treasure. Of course I grant there is the spiritual side of things, love and all that. We try to love our children for a few hours each day, to stabilize them. I advise you, Toby, to take up some kind of profitable business as soon as you can. But I wish—

She fell quiet, not speaking her wish, and looked into the cradle. Toby looked too, and saw Chicks as a little girl, fast asleep, with her eyes closed upon a future dream of a vast world, changing and sucked and warm, like an aniseed ball.

Then he turned to Daphne who was rocking her cradle and crooning something which sounded like,

> Sift where and how through a cloud of sky
> Brown the green sea in a warm salt pie,
> Eat and turn off the sun and die
> Cold as a coin in an oven of why.

She stopped singing and rocking and stared past Toby to something beyond him. He looked over his shoulder, afraid, and saw a vaporous and profound drop of nothing.

—Toby, Daphne said. We have dug the pit and he who diggeth the pit shall fall into it; but that is only Francie, the witch who dug fire; and Chicks, Teresa now, has filled the pit with silver and copper and gold and three children and Timothy Harlow, and builds a house over the pit, to live there; and I, Daphne, live unburned in the centre, brought to the confusion of dream; and you, Toby, are there and not there, journeying half-way which is all torment for

> *The singe on the sleeve is worse than fire*
> *The half-place than the knowing where,*
> *Like seas between to the unhappy sailor.*
> *Poor trafficking child, with no treasure.*

Then Toby watched the three of them dancing and rocking the cradles and chanting, and changing from Francie and Daphne and Chicks, to bony women shrieking Aii-aii-aii, louder, with faces now like a clock, luminous, and numbered to twelve, and hair standing up, tingling like a five o'clock alarm. Then silence and dark, and a wavery wobble of a new bird waking up outside in the white pear tree.

23

In the morning he did not remember his dream for like most dreams his memory of it ended with—I dreamt something last night, I don't know what, it was queer, something about a telescope and a pie, I think it was an apple pie cooking in an oven.

He was saying this at breakfast, over bacon and eggs and fried bread, with the yolk of the egg bleeding over his plate and his mother saying, glancing sideways from dishing out her husband's breakfast and putting it in the top shelf of the oven to warm, and his slippers on the bottom shelf,

—Oh Toby, I didn't know I hadn't cooked it enough.

Toby hadn't noticed either, till his mother called his attention from his dream to his flowing half-cooked egg; and he scolded in the way he had learned from his father.

—Haven't I told you before, to leave the egg till it's wrinkled on top and hard, that I don't like them runny?

And then, his dream reabsorbing him, he added,

—Yes, something about an apple pie cooking in an oven, and I was looking in my Atlas, at the different countries. I think I was on the moon.

—Little wonder, said Amy, this morning's paper talks of the moon, and visiting there. Shares have gone up for holiday resorts on the moon. That's what your father says.

Amy Withers did not read the paper herself. She seemed not to have time. Her husband was up in the dumpy and she had settled his breakfast and was nursing the warmed teapot, waiting for the kettle, and conscious through the blue smoke and sizzle of the old day after day despair of not managing and letting the eggs be runny, and forgetting to give the fowls water. Talk of a dream, and the words apple pie and atlas and moon came to her, visiting, like consoling friends in her perpetual bereavement of cooking and muddle; from her own world long stifled, of unreal and might-have-been. She seized the words, apple pie, dream, moon, and with them knitted herself a warm half-minute escape from the forever problem of facing up.

—Toby, she said, that means travel. I think it means much travel for many years. And how strange about apple pie, because Dad brought up some of those fillbaskets from the shed, and I had planned to have apple pie, a real old-fashioned one for tea either tonight or tomorrow night.

She looked suspiciously at Toby.

—You didn't *know* I was having apple pie for tea, did you? Nobody told you?

—Have a heart, Mum. And so I'm going to travel many miles in many years.

He looked at his mother with her shrunken dangling breasts and her thin time and child-stolen lap and her fixed expression of agreement and comfort and faith that had settled about her mouth, belied by the fear and loneliness that flowed round and round, at times, in a capture, within her faded blue eyes; and he *knew* just as he *knew* that he knew his dream of the corner of the moon but could not utter it, that his mother in her life of cooking and washing and going messages and visiting the sick with flowers and home-made cakes; and sitting on Sunday, saying special grace—Bless this food to our use and us in Thy keeping—or reading the Bible and breaking bread, with her eyes on the invisible Jesus who said, Take. Eat. This is my body.

In all her living Toby knew that his mother, who had never left her native land nor had a holiday from home, had indeed experienced what she foresaw for him,

Much travel in many years,

so that her shoes wore out and her feet bulged over the sides, and her slippers, men's size, suffered split heels and toes. She had corns, one or two, which she cut at night with a razor-blade, in the steaming bathroom; and flat feet, fallen arches, they were called; and varicose veins as if she had walked her life through Europe and Asia and South Africa and America and India; when all the time it was in her own backyard and garden of beans and cabbages and carrot seed that never came up for the wind breathed a blow-a-way spell.

—Yes, you will travel, Toby, I'm sure of it. I said you would dream of your future, though I don't believe the superstition.

—I don't know if it was my future I dreamt of, Mum; it seemed my past.

His mother smiled.

—They are the same, Toby. It is the same thing with a different name.

But how he hated her when she smiled that apostolic way, as if she were in league with God and time, if there were a god; as if she were a chosen being, which perhaps she was, but it made him angry and guilty to think so, for then should he not clothe her in silk and satin, and give her breakfast in bed, instead of her fetching breakfast for him; and say to her each time she waited upon him,

—Let *me* do that, mother. You just sit by the fire and rest.

Should he not act this way? And what if, as she grew older, she began to wander, and do strange things and went blind? What should he do? Should he put her in a home, and visit her once a week with oranges and violets or some other flower, perhaps take her for a drive down to see the breakers coming in; or shout her an ice-cream if the weather were warm? Or keep her home, employ a nurse to look after her, and have her wandering and tottering everywhere and interfering and taking up time and money that he had slaved for, to make his adult treasure? And about his father, what should he do about his father when *he* grew older and got deaf as Grandad had been, to be shouted at and explained to; when he quavered and tottered and dribbled and wet his pants and smelt? It was all terrible, Toby thought. He could not face it. He would have his hands full to control the treasure of money that would help him to fit in and know where and why and how.

He did not know, then, what to do, and wondered why he had thought about it all. Because his mother interpreted his dream much travel in many years. And can you not travel, in a dead and suffocating way, merely standing still?

—Toby, there's a bit more fried bread, if you want it.

—No thanks.

He was a bit of fried bread himself, he fancied, sitting soaked up in his dream.

24

For three months, then, until Christmas, Toby worked to demolish the old Peterkin Hotel. His father helped him, not at first or ever because he wanted to, but because Toby, coming home one night tired and dusty with limestone as if someone had waited in the dark to empty over him a bag of dirty wholemeal flour, said bitterly to his mother,

—Look at Dad there. What do you see?

His mother looked but did not answer. Bob was slumped asleep with his detective novel fallen on the floor and his mouth open, dirty and dark red, like a drain. His bottom teeth were decayed. He ought to have had them seen to.

—Pure laziness, Toby said. While I slave all day trying to earn money to set me up in business. Why can't he help me from time to time? If I don't get some money I shall have to sell out my share of the house, and then where will you both go?

—Yes, thought Amy. Then where will we go?

She was used to Toby's threats but they frightened her, and muddled her, as she tried to think of some place to go, a *where* that would be the answer to all worries and bickerings, and bring peace. Surely the Bible talks of some place, she thought. Surely the Bible will help, and praying, for we're not young any more and can't think so quickly, nor can I walk a few yards now but I have to stop and get my lost breath.

—You wouldn't sell out, Toby. Not with your mother and father getting old?

—Of course I wouldn't sell out. Not of my *own* accord. But I may be *forced* to, if things go as they are, if that lazy heap doesn't help me get the building down in time.

—Toby. Your father isn't a lazy heap. He's retired. It's the twilight of his life.

Bob Withers woke up suddenly. He tasted in his mouth and sniffed and picked up the book from the hearthrug. *The Strange Murder of Hogden Park*. Then,

—What's going on, he said. What are you arguing about, always arguing about something. And why isn't the weather on, you know I hate to miss the weather report.

Amy Withers did not say—You would have been asleep and not heard it, but obediently switched the radio on and it sang at them.

When the sun in the morning looks over the hill
and kisses the flowers on mocking-bird hill.

—Missed it, said Bob Withers accusingly. Turn it off.

Every day he liked to hear the weather report. He scorned the weather-man, and laughed at him because he spoke with a marble in his mouth, and besides, Bob could tell at a glance whether the next day would be fine or wet; but he felt that nowadays it was the thing to be *told*, and have everything worked out for you. Hearing the weather report made Bob feel safe, in the otherwise insecure and frightening times that he called, in opposition to the old days, modern times, nowadays, these days.

—Now, he said, who's to tell if there'll be a storm or hurricane or the world will break tomorrow into a million pieces? I like to know my future. I'm not altogether superstitious, but I like to know my future, so as to be sure.

—I'm selling out my share, Dad. Unless you can help me with the Peterkin. Surely you can help for a few days at least?

Amy looked from one to the other, supporting both but unable to decide what to say. She fixed a calm hopeful expression on her face, but fear sneaked in and out of her eyes. She was tired. Blessed are the peacemakers, she thought.

—What do you say, Mum?

—Yes, what do you say, Mum?

Amy smiled with her familiar mask of brightness.

—I'll say it's time for a cup of tea, a real cup of tea, and one of the coconut cakes I made this afternoon.

Tea? Coconut cakes? Take your pick, Bob would say teasingly as he helped himself from the plate. But he loved coconut cakes.

So Amy settled the dispute, and the next morning Bob went down with Toby in the truck to the Peterkin Hotel.

Bob didn't know about pulling down buildings and had to be told. Do this, Dad, Toby would say. Do that. And Bob obeyed meekly. It's funny, he thought, I didn't realise Toby was grown-up and knew things. I always thought, oh I don't know what I always thought. And he saw a sick little boy with his left eye screwed up and his head twisted over his left shoulder, and crying, Dad, Dad, help me 'cos you *know*.

And standing there on the scaffolding high above the people passing in the street, with Toby on one end of the board, hammering and wrenching, and himself at the other end, also hammering, but with the inferior hammer, Toby had the better one with the claw because, after all, it was Toby's job, and Toby was the craftsman, Bob felt sometimes tired and out of breath, it was when he raised his arms, and giddy, and that was when he looked down at the people walking; but he could not tell Toby about his feelings. And he felt lonely so close up to the sky, not the rewarding and proud loneliness he had felt when driving the train at night across the plains, but an unforgiving and harsh emptiness, as if he had been rejected by earth and sky and must stay forever now in the between gulf, tired and afraid. And from the street, if people looked up as people do, craning their necks and stopping, blocking up the footpath, they saw two dusty and shabbily dressed men, one young, the other old, standing at each end of a paint-smattered plank, turning sometimes to glance at each other, but rarely speaking; as if they played there, had the board been moving, in an enclosure of sky, a grim and aloof game of private see-saw.

Toby enjoyed demolishing the building. The place, he felt, was his possession. He would dismember it and make it pay. He ripped up the floor and found with delight what lay underneath, old newspapers and sixpences and haircombs; teaspoons, and a broken wrist watch; a faded portrait of a woman smiling. And he explored the linings of the walls to find treasure. He thought, I will reduce the place to chaos and

out of the neat stacks of timber and glass and blocks of limestone create a new and personal wealth that will be my friend
and lover for the rest of my life. So. The rusty nails and the
borer-riddled four-by-two and the kauri beams and the sheets
of roofing iron—more than any Fay Chalklin.

In three months, two weeks before Christmas, the building
was finished and the place where it had been rooted resembled
the socket of a giant wood and stone tooth, a pioneer molar;
the place of dark blood to be filled and healed with bright
green weed. Perhaps. Or a false tooth? And that it proved to
be, shooting up early the following year; a hardware store,
an advertisement of its own destruction, with axes and saws
and shears and mowers planted behind the receding plate-
glass windows. And next door a milk bar was born, clean and
white and shining, with sweets in bottles and two kinds of ice
cream, plain and chocolate; and a nickelodeon that agreed
on payment to sing the latest tunes. And people said, who
had lived in Waimaru for many years,
   —How the town progresses!

25

       The radio began it all first, threatening and remem-
bering. The newspapers followed with their insinuations of
panic. The shops repeated the dreadful declaration and warning.
   —Not many days to Christmas, they said. Have *you* posted
      your cards and parcels? Have *you* finished Christmas
      shopping?
The shops in town were made into homes for old men with
long white beards and dressing-gowns and gumboots and
falsely or not so falsely red noses. The world snowed cottonwool
and sprouted tender pine trees and sullen holly leaves; stars
fell from heaven and were confusedly followed by numerous
magi; in the best shop windows appeared mangers, centrally-
heated, all awaiting a *birth certainly*.
   —Christmas, sighed Amy Withers in rapture. Christmas.
First, the cards. Bob bought them from Woolworths, at the
threepenny counter, complete with envelope, and Amy made
out the list of addresses.
   —Of course we'll send one to the Thomson's, she said.
   —But they didn't send us one last year.

—But what if they send us one this year and we haven't bought one for them?

—We can buy them a New Year card instead. Or a calendar.

—But then they'll know we didn't think to buy them a card.

—Oh well, send them one, said Bob. Only another three-pence. I'm made of money. We can afford anything, anything in the world. Where do you get all these people to send cards to? Who's this D. Taylor, anyway?

—That's an old friend of mine, Dad. She went to school with me. We always send each other a card at Christmas. We've never missed in all these years.

—Funny, I can't remember her, said Bob.

—You didn't know her, Dad. I've known many people that you didn't know, just as you've known people too.

—But I don't keep up with them, Bob said, lonely. I haven't kept up with any of them.

So the cards were sent, ones with words like bless and love and cheer, and verses that were not cheating and modern but really rhyming so you could see the rhymes.

Next, the parcels. For Daphne (poor soul, they said) a pair of pink fleecy-lined bloomers with elastic in the legs; a matching pink petticoat from Woolworths; and a box of chocolates. And a note enclosed, which said, Dear Daphne, A very happy Christmas and a prosperous New Year and God bless you. We should like to come and visit you but the doctor thinks you are not just well enough, but perhaps next Christmas we hope to have you with us to share in the blessings of the Lord. The cats, Fyodor and Matilda are very well. There's nothing more I can think of to say except have faith and God bless you. Your loving mother in the hope of Christ, Amy Withers.

Next, for Chicks (Mum, *do* remember that I am Teresa now that I am married and grown-up) there was the excitement of buying for the children. Toys to send north. A plastic fish for the baby; a magnet for each of the two little boys. Bob Withers spent all evening playing with the magnet, picking up pins which he had scattered over the kitchen table; saying, Got it, Got it; and We never had things like this when we were young. He also played with the glove puppets, the policeman whose right hand was a truncheon, and the poor bedraggled sinner with stupid face and striped gown; beating the wrongdoer with the truncheon, mercilessly, twisting both puppets into strange postures, dancing them about the kitchen table until Amy laughed,

—Oh Dad, your antics, she said. You're nothing but a child. Won't it be lovely when Chicks and Tim and the kiddies come south to live, and we can see them; it'll be like childhood over again.

—I don't want childhood over again, said Bob, beating with his truncheon at the sinner who cried down tears of red paint, I don't want childhood again.

Toby, who was lying on the sofa half-asleep, said

—I suppose I'll have a pack of screaming kids coming and running wild over my gear and stuff down the drive?

Toby, having finished his Peterkin Hotel deal had applied for and been granted a licence for dealing in secondhand goods. He bought and sold bottles and rags and scrap iron, old bedsteads, stoves, anything old and used. Sometimes he visited the town rubbish dump, not the old dump with its circle of toi-toi—that had been filled in and a new house built upon it—but the other place on the outskirts of the town near the mouth of the river. The Shingle Tip. Sometimes Toby would drive his truck out to the tip and sit at the wheel watching the sea and river meet, the trout-brown water spread out like a lap across the smooth ivory stones; and the hesitant sea, reinforced with tide, saying hush hush hush to its own talking; and creeping up, first in small pools filled with gift of shell and sea-leaves, then in long chain of white and green dance, closing upon the river, snuffling under and sighing for the now brown and yellow petticoat of foam and the wasted weed and the slow stifling calm of a green-brown half-place. Hush-hush. Hush-sh-sh-sh.

If only the sea would stop for a second or minute or five minutes enough to give man a word or cry or song or curse in edgeways.

And as Toby sat there in the truck with the sea inhabiting his ear, he would say, irritably,

—Shut up. Keep quiet while I think.

—*What will you think about, Toby?*

—Oh, about things in general.

—*What specific things, Toby?*

—Oh, don't pin me down to details. Anything.

—*What will you think about, Toby? What will you think?*

—Keep flowing then, and be damned. *But speak for me.*

26

The hollow house will never be filled.

The Christmas cards are propped along the mantelpiece; the sixpenny lights like blatant outsize boiled sweets, red, gold, and berry-blue, twist and squirm on the ceiling; the concertina bells that sigh when the breeze from outside snuffs at them, are settled and specked with flies that sit close, like black millions of people on a paper world; streamers and thin paper Santas hung by the neck with spangle, loop from wall to wall of kitchen; a dying branch of pine leans tired upon the bookcase, rows of calendars hide, face to the wall, in shame, till the first of January, promising their glory of rose and lily and sea and sunset and hunted stag; the bitter sprigs of holly dig for spite through the faded wallpaper.

And the hollow house will never be filled.

It is Christmas Day, three o'clock in the afternoon. Toby and Bob Withers are sprawled asleep on sofa and armchair. Amy has just finished washing the dinner dishes and putting away the remains of the roast lamb and the dark half-eaten earth of plum pudding, dropping, as she opens the door of the safe that hangs outside under the pear tree, a few scraps of meat for the cats, Fyodor and Matilda. Puss puss. Puss puss. But Fyodor and Matilda are far far too sleepy to uncurl from their breathing black and grey cloud. Everything drowses, why not we, say Fyodor and Matilda. The sun covers his face with soft white and grey paw and the few kittens of cloud uncurl yawn and curl up again. Puss puss indeed.

And *O little town of Bethlehem, Come All Ye Faithful*, sings the Ladies' Choir, specially chosen, over the radio.

Amy walks to the window and looks down the path. I thought I heard someone coming, a car. I'll give them a piece of shortbread or Christmas cake for afternoon tea. But I hope it's not visitors. I'll just put the cloth over the table to keep the flies away from the cake and go and have a lie-down in the front room.

She takes off her slippers, new, tartan, shaped like rowing boats, and lies down upon the bed in the front room.

Behold a virgin shall be with child

and shall bring forth a son
and they shall call his name Emmanuel
which being interpreted is God with us
and because iniquity shall abound the love of many shall
    wax cold
but he that endure unto the end, the same shall be saved.
And many other texts did Amy repeat to herself, staring at the fly-specked ceiling and the dressing-table opposite with its clutter of old bills and photos and Bob's handkerchiefs, dirty from his smoker's cough; and Amy's bottle of heart pills, and Bob's liver pills; and the large green comb, like a rake, that gathered grey hair in its teeth, and was never cleaned; and then Amy's bottom teeth that she never wore because they never fitted. And Amy with her head upon the dirty pillow-case—she has given the clean one to Bob for his side of the bed—finds herself crying, and she turns her face to the pillow smelling the dusty flock and the stopped smell of years, and she forgets about Christmas and the cake being watched all afternoon when it was baked a fortnight ago, and the power getting cut off, and her fear of failure, for oh the expense of things like crystallised cherries and almonds and nuts and lemon peel; and she forgets Christmas Eve with the carols over the radio and Bob sitting reading his detective book and saying, —When can we get something decent on the air instead of that infernal singing; and Toby, her only son, out down the street to walk there alone and see the Pipe Band Parade and make sure to get his new supply of pills; and the family waking on Christmas morning with pretence of surprise at their presents.

—Socks, socks, Bob had said. Now how on earth did Santa
    know I needed socks?

And he had bought them himself, of course, and the other presents. The three of them knew there was no surprise and the morning was really old and frayed, like a purse ransacked of wonder.

Except for Christ, of course, Amy had thought guiltily. For the people walking in darkness, have they not seen a great light?

So she lies on her bed, crying, and remembering, how strange, something that will not be put out of her mind. Just something silly and small, long ago. How she worked for the magistrate and his wife, cleaning their house and waiting on

93

the table. Dressed in a black dress with white cuffs. And Mrs Togbetty said one morning,

—Amy Amy can you clean a fowl? Mr Togbetty is having a party and I want you to clean a fowl.

And Amy had gone out in the backyard to clean the fowl, plucking first, with feathers everywhere and the tips of her fingers sore, and a feather down her throat, until the fowl lay naked and pale yellow with an everlasting shiver.

And then Mrs Togbetty said,

—Amy Amy will you bath the dog?

And Amy put a big apron round her dress and went again into the backyard and bathed the cheeky little spaniel dog. And that night Mr Togbetty had a party. He wore a wig partly because he was bald, and partly because he was a magistrate, and inside the wig he stuffed a piece of cottonwool to keep his head warm.

—Amy Amy, he said, is my wig straight?

Amy said that his wig was straight.

And he had his party while Amy had the evening off.

—You can go anywhere you like, they said.

It was too far to go home so Amy walked up and down the streets, with her hatpin in her pocket in case a man made advances to her; and she sat for a while by the river that flowed through the town, and she looked at the fallen poplar leaves and thought how sad. How sad and lonely. And she sat there until darkness came and the mist seeming like smoke from the smouldering leaves and she looked down at the penny-glint of water and up at the burrowing mass of sky and thought, Something wonderful is going to happen. I can feel it. This night is a special night.

She walked back to the Togbettys and in the gate and up the path past the window where Mr Togbetty was entertaining his friends. She heard them talking and laughing. There was a small space at the window where the blind had not been pulled down and she peeped in, with a trembling of excitement. After all, it was a *real* party.

They were playing cards. She could see their hands and the cards, but mostly the big drawing room table with the red velvet cover, thick, like a carpet laid out for a queen, and rich, like a dark rose.

She could not see any more of the party. The laughing and talking and people were secret behind the blind and curtain,

and all her share was the soft crimson cloth with the white
hands dancing the cards upon it.

And that night she cried herself to sleep for disappointment
and loneliness.

And now Amy, lying upon her bed on Christmas afternoon,
cannot help seeing over and over again the red tablecloth that
was her share of the party; and the tablecloth grows bigger
and falls upon her bed and covers her like a blanket and she
sleeps.

And the hollow house will never be filled.

27

CHICKS

*And now Daphne in the dead room has taken
the small stone cup of sun poured through the high-up
window; and split the gold mass to wheat, and feeds the
white fowls hurrying hither and thither upon the grass,
and feeds the littlest chickens too, though these not
knowing the grass yet but whispering underneath the box
with the warm feathery mother hen.*
*And chook chook chook Daphne calls, scattering the wheat,
and the fowls say quark quark quark, and flap their feathers
in the dusty places, picking water too, dipping their beaks
into the rusty pan of clear creek-water, clicking their top and
bottom of beak together, like people tasting their false teeth
and being polite about it and not opening their mouths;
then pointing their beak to the sky for the creek-water to
trickle down in a clear thread.*
*—What finesse of tasting, sings Daphne, laughing today.
But crying too, for the littlest chicken, like wattle, under
the big dark box, not being able to see, while the pale-combed
broody hen tiptoes in the sun for the first time of sleep in
a tired life, in the place coloured brown, with the white shroud
apron up to the neck and the warm pikelet or muffin of
dung in the underneath mouth.*

95

28

Toby found the diary under a cushion in the sitting room up north. He was staying the night with Chicks (Teresa now) and Timothy, and was looking after the children while their parents were visiting the home of a friend.

—A business friend, Toby, and business friends cannot be ignored. You don't mind looking after the children, Toby? They never wake. You need not go near them.

So Toby sat on the sofa in the front room of the flash house. And there he found the diary and read it, first with a feeling of guilt, later with no feeling but death and shame. He read—
January 15th

For the first time in many years, eight years ago to be exact, since it is eight years ago that I married, I have decided to keep a diary. I intend to put in it all my feelings and every happening of importance. Indeed I think I shall be very frank, like the Frenchman, Rousseau, and put in everything. Or nearly everything. I intend to give, perhaps, if I have time, a brief account of my life in my eight years of marriage. Perhaps I shall refer to my childhood and the members of my family, my brother Toby who is a licenced second-hand dealer in Waimaru, my sister Daphne who is in a mental hospital, my other sister Francie who was burned when I was quite small. And my mother and father. Naturally I shall talk of Timothy and the children. I am determined to keep this diary regularly, and if it happens that I miss a few days it will not mean that I have forgotten to record incidents and emotions, only that I have not found time; after all, I am a housewife.

Now where shall I begin? I do not know. I shall put this away until after the children have gone to bed.
Night

Timothy (I shall call him Timothy because it sounds more bookish and sophisticated) is amused that I should have begun a diary, and he threatens to read it, yet dear Timothy, he is so honest that I could leave it lying anywhere in the house and he would never open it. No, I believe I shall write of my husband as Tim—the other sounds too much like a stranger. He has given me a steam iron. He brought it home tonight as a surprise. I shall give my old one to Daphne so that when she recovers she will have some kind of material basis for her new life.

Now to really begin my diary.

In August or October we shall be going south to Waimaru, to live. I am excited and afraid to visit the scene of my birth and childhood. It is like returning to the place of crime, but it will be spring and all the blossoms and daffodils will have budded. I long to see them. I remember a poem we had at school, about daffodils fluttering

> beside the lake, beneath the trees.

I should like to put in a simile, the way it is done by writers, to describe the loveliness of the blossoms in my old home. I can think of nothing to say except they are choking white.

Even now I have not really begun my diary. I like my name, Teresa, and if people at home when I visit there prefer to call me Chicks, I shall refuse to answer. They used to call me Chicks because, they said, I was like a little dark chicken running about, trying to catch up with people, and almost pecking for grains of wheat upon the ground, with my head down and the hair falling over my face. My other sisters had interesting names. There was Francie, that was Frances, and though she wore slacks and my father seemed angry with her, I thought she was some relation to Saint Francis who, I believed, kept animals in his pocket and took them out and licked them, the way Francie licked a blackball or acid drop, for pure love. And there is Daphne who, I thought, smelt like a flower bush, half-way between lilac and catmint. And Toby, my brother, who had no particular smell that I remember. He wore braces. Children nowadays wear belts, men too. I should laugh and laugh if I saw Tim hitching up his pants with a pair of braces. He wears action-waist. I gave him a pair for Christmas and he gave me a set of nylon underwear, the sort that breathes, blue, with wide lace at the edges. I love Christmas with the children waking earlier than light and climbing into bed between Tim and me, showing us their presents and snuggling down for a new sleep. What hot little bodies they have, and bright eyes and fresh voices, why, they shine with newness. And Who puts the sun out? Peter asks me, as if I should know. The dark is a frightening answer.

January 16th

The washing machine has leaked over the floor. And the baby Sharon is sick with her teeth. She cried all night and her little right cheek is flushed like a cherry. Why cannot children be born with teeth?

January 20th

It is almost the end of the first month of a new year. I feel I have done nothing, though what I should be doing I do not know, it is just the feeling of getting nowhere and of time passing. I shall be twenty-eight this year, nearly thirty, then forty, and then come the fifties and sixties, why in no time I shall be an old woman collecting an old age pension. I am afraid to think of it. Why, it will happen in almost no time. My own mother is old and ill, they say she will die soon with her heart. I shall get old like her and have high blood pressure and varicose veins and dropsy and have to squeeze the salt out of every pound of butter and remember not to put salt in the vegetables or on lettuce or any food because it is forbidden. Or perhaps I shall get diabetes like my grandmother, and not eat sugar, and have my legs taken off, to be kept behind the door in the dark.

Enough of this morbid writing. It just happens that I seem to be doing the same thing over and over every day—get up, get dressed, get the breakfast, dress the children, Peter and Mark, or pester them till they dress themselves, send them out to play, give baby her bottle and put her down to sleep, have a peaceful cup of tea—that means a cup of tea in peace—with Tim before he goes off to work, wash the dishes, vacuum the carpets, turn on the washing-machine, wash, rinse, spin-dry, hang out the washing, sit down to morning tea with the paper to read and the scandal.

And so on and on. In the afternoon I have time to read. I am reading *The Tenant of Wildfell Hall* by Anne Brontë. It is the story of a woman and her drunkard husband, her suffering and terror in a world of squalor—that is what it says on the cover. I find the book absorbing, indeed I dare not put it down. What will Huntingdon do next, I ask myself, quivering, like his wife Helen, for fear and suspense. What a brute of a man to so treat a woman's love. The scene where Huntingdon has a rendezvous in the shrubbery with his current mistress, and his wife, taking a solitary walk in the same area at nightfall, is mistaken by Huntingdon for the woman he has promised to meet, and therefore greeted passionately and fondled, until he discovers his error and exclaims in disgust and fear, —My wife! Helen!

that scene abhorrs and disgusts me. I have read it carefully three times.

Sometimes in the afternoon I have visitors like the Baldwins, Benny and Ted, or the Smarts, Terry and Josie. Very often Benny and Josie call and we sit and talk babies and husbands and housework over a cup of tea and biscuits. I feel so ashamed that I never have tins full of my own cooking when visitors call—I have to undo the cellophane off packets of biscuits, chocolate and wafers, and pasties; and though Benny and Josie are too polite to make remarks, I feel their criticism, for they always have meringues or peanut brownies or those pinky marshmallow cakes, when I visit them. Benny's father is a judge in the Supreme Court and her husband is high-up in the Civil Service. The Smarts have a new house over in one of the bays—a coming area, they say. They know the Bessicks, Dr Herbert and his wife Alison, and have promised us an introduction. Dr Bessick is a brilliant gynaecologist, just returned from studying overseas—his wife had an article in the social news about their life on the continent and the States. She is a bit of a shrew, they say, but dresses perfectly and is, they say, an entertaining hostess. Both the Baldwins and the Smarts, by the way, are in the local drama club. We have playreadings on Tuesdays.

Now how else shall I describe my day? In the evening after tea there is always the children's bath and story, for Tim and I believe in the idea of putting children to bed after a story. Tim bought a book on child psychology, and we have studied it. Some of the ideas do not seem to work with Mark, he is so individual and temperamental. Tim reads the story while I fix the baby's bottle. Childrens books are different now from when I was a child. I have enjoyed reading *Jemima Puddleduck*, by Beatrix Potter, I had never read it before, how the foxy gentleman kept his newspaper in his tail coat pocket and had a shed full of feathers for Jemima Puddleduck to lay her eggs in. What a cunning swindler was the foxy gentleman, and how gullible poor Jemima Puddleduck. It was almost like real life with its intrigue and near-murder.

By the way, Tim has bought me an electric cake mixer so that I can make a chocolate and walnut sponge for the weekend when we meet the Bessicks. It'll be strange to meet a doctor socially, especially a gynaecologist, though I shall be too seasoned to blush if I remember what he must know about the insides of women. Ten years ago I should have fled. Just imagine.

It is late now and I am tired. Tim has just gone down to the gate with the milk bottles. Oh, the weather is so hot and humid, I don't know how I can bear it sometimes. And the mosquitoes, there seems to be a plague of them this year—they say there have never been so many. I shall go to bed soon. Benny says she uses Wisteria Night Cream, that it is better than Gloria Haven. I have tried Gloria Haven before and I, too, feel there is something lacking in it. Today I bought a pot of Wisteria at the chemist's, extravagance no doubt, but Tim does not mind, indeed he encourages me, and likes to see me taking an interest in my make-up. What a perfect husband. Where in all the world would I find a man more thoughtful or loving? And to think that years ago he was one of those dirty little boys who used to hang around my sister Francie at Waimaru, and I used to poke my tongue out at him. His father was a council man, and though Tim began his first year medical, he did not finish it, it was not suited to his talents. He is now high-up in selling, not a mere commercial traveller, but a high pressure executive with responsibility. His friend Howard Weston (the Westons have a sheep station in the country back of Waimaru) has fixed the sale of our new house at Waimaru. When I saw the pictures and plans of it, I thought it seemed strange that it should be built over the old rubbish dump where we used to play as children and where Francie was burned. The idea frightened me. Living where we used to sit amongst the toi-toi, tickling it down our backs and putting it in our hair for feathers; where we explored and found what we called treasure, old tyres and boots that we said were walked in at night by dead men and giants; and bits of motor cars, and books, and all the rubbish under the sun. And from morning to night, how long seemed the time, with the day taking chicken steps in the sky. Yes, when I live in our house there I shall feel afraid and strange; yet I feel it is the right place to live; the place with its promise of happiness and treasure in our future life and then its despair over Francie, I had a blue ribbon in my hair that day, and it kept coming undone and there was no one to tie it for me; it is like a kind of gap in my life. What nonsense I talk.

Now I must stop writing in this diary for tonight. Tim is in the bath. He always runs it far too hot so that the place is all steam and his body like a cooked crayfish; and he even *reads* in the bath. Dear Tim! To think I have been married eight years. Now I must go to bed, and before I sleep, finish one more chapter of *The Tenant of Wildfell Hall*.

January 21st

I am excited over meeting the Bessicks. And afraid. It will be my first *real* experience of hostessing to people who really matter. I have asked them to come in the evening for I think it would be more convenient and less nerve-racking with the children asleep, though I had wanted to show off Sharon's curly hair and dimples and that charming smile of hers, and the pink nylon frock, embroidered in Switzerland. Never mind. To fill in a little of the evening, if conversation lags, we have arranged to play Beethoven's Fifth Symphony on the radiogram. I am quite safe with that for I have read about it and what it is meant to represent and know the different movements, and therefore should be able to make some intelligent remark about it. I believe the Bessicks are musical, and I feel quite safe with the Fifth Symphony. I can mention about fate knocking on the door and that kind of thing. I shall do out the sitting-room in the afternoon so as to have it ready, and make the sponge in the morning. I have decided on coffee sponge instead of chocolate as coffee is more intellectual. I shall wear a simple tasteful frock of taffeta, with my new gipsy earrings, and my hair done as usual with the parting slightly higher. It ought to settle if I wash it the night before, Friday night, or perhaps two nights before, Thursday, and then it will be manageable.

You must forgive me for writing all this, but it absorbs me, you know. They say Herbert Bessick is unique.

January 22nd

Hot weather still. The children are running around bare. I had a letter from Daphne today, the first for a long time. What a strange world she must be living in! Her letter does not make sense, it is a wonder the doctor let it be posted— all about Christmas and a piece of moon and a mouse nibbling at a shroud of sun, it frightens me, I can never see her getting better and living a normal life like myself. Poor Daphne. And she sends back the letter I wrote her, and has written the words Help help help at the end of my letter. As if I had to be rescued from a terrible doom, as if fate (I think of the

Fifth Symphony) knocked at my door. Poor Daphne. Naturally she means herself when she cries help help help.

January 23rd

Only three more days. I am as excited as a young girl going to her first party. I remember my first party, a sixth form one, at school, when the high school boys were invited and I had nothing decent to wear, while the other girls were dressed in the loveliest frocks, evening gowns or ones ballerina length, with satin slippers, and holding evening bags covered with sparkly beads. The party was held in the gymnasium, I remember, and I sat all night, ashamed of my plain print dress, and being afraid to talk to anyone. And when the dances were announced my heart beat so fast I was afraid it would choke me, like in a novel, and I would fall swooning to the ground. But who could ever swoon in a print frock and wearing walking shoes, lace-ups? I waited for someone to ask me to dance. The boy Tod came up and asked me if I was engaged for the next dance, a foxtrot, and I said in a rush—No, I'll dance with you, and I grabbed him and pushed him onto the floor, and we danced; but I could not keep in time, and trod on his toes, and said Sorry sorry, all the time, though I learned afterwards that a woman never says sorry—it is always the man's fault. I did not know what to talk about while we danced, I was too busy trying to keep in step and show my partner what a good dancer I was, in the hope that he would ask me for supper. He was captain of the cricket eleven.

He didn't ask me for supper. Nobody did. I could have wept, and I knew it was all the fault of my funny clothes and not being able to afford dancing lessons. And I had to go to supper with the rest of the girls that were left over, and we sat together at a long table while the others with partners sat at tables for two, and talked and laughed in an intimate way, while we girls sat angry and silent or else looking haughty, pretending it did not matter—but it did matter.

But to return to the present time. I am really excited about Saturday. I love to think that I have some kind of social standing, enough for the Bessicks to want to meet Tim and me. I have finished *The Tenant of Wildfell Hall* and have begun *Wuthering Heights*, by Emily Brontë. I read it years ago when I was a schoolgirl and in search of some kind of romance. My reading of it now will be more mature and balanced.

Peter is full of the quaintest remarks. He said this morning—Mummy, what kind of a world is the world in the washing machine? And last night he asked about the moon. There's something in it, he said. Like hills, and something that moves. He is in primer three at school, and anxious for the holidays to finish. I see myself as the mother of a Rhodes Scholar.

But it is night and I am very tired. The children seem to have been squabbling all day over toy ducks and guns and motor-cars until I am weary of the sound of their voices. And Sharon has diarrhoea, so I have to wash a million nappies. I thank heaven for a washing machine. Poor Sharon. I laugh now to think of Mark, and how I was scared of him at first, he was so tiny and slippery, and how carefully I washed his ears and mouth and nose with cotton wool and his body with olive oil, and crept in the room at night to see if he had stopped breathing or had smothered by putting his face in the pillow, the way you see it reported in the newspapers. Dear Mark. How terrible if any of them had been born blind or deformed or idiots that waved their heads around, like caterpillars, and never learned to speak.

Now I will finish this record for the night. I have told you I am tired.

I have just remembered that Herbert Bessick spent some time in France, and he speaks French well, they say. We learned French at school, a little, from a French tutor. How wonderful if I could speak French with him at the party.

Correction; it is not a party, just a quiet social evening.

January 24th

I had a strange dream last night. I dreamt I was sitting in the middle of the arena at a circus, nursing a little black panther that kept scratching at me and saying in a child's voice with a foreign accent—I'll scratch your eyes out. I'll scratch your eyes out.

The spotlights of the circus played over me, and though I knew I was expected to perform in some way, I found that I could not remember my act. The audience in the big top cheered and stamped and whistled, waiting for me to begin. Suddenly I threw the panther away from me across the ring and began to cry, and I thought, This is only a dream, there is nothing to cry about, it is just a dream. Then the light in the circus faded and I found myself in Paris, walking by the Seine river. It was midnight. I heard a clock striking twelve, and I kept on walking looking down at my shadow cast in the water to make sure it was walking with me. Suddenly I felt tired and knew I must sleep, so I took off my black fur coat—thinking, how strange, I did not notice I wore a black fur coat—and spread it on the ground and fell asleep on it. When I awoke my fur coat had vanished, my shadow had vanished, I was standing staring in the river that swirled in a whirlpool of darkness.

Now isn't that a weird dream? I asked Tim if he dreamt a dream last night, and he said no, except at one time he half dreamt he was climbing a mountain to find an orchid, but found only a handful of snow. Dreams are curious things. They say that dreams mean more than people think.

By the way, when I first began this diary I said I would give a record of my inner life. I begin to wonder if I have said anything about my inner life. What if I have *no inner life*? I am morbid today. I had a letter from my mother in Waimaru. She says the same thing over and over in her letters; that everything is well, that everybody is happy; and she says it like a chant of denial, so that you can't help knowing that nothing is well, and nobody is happy. Sometimes I wonder if we should go south to live. I don't know. I really don't know.

Today and tomorrow and then the day of my little social gathering. I am beginning to wonder if I should make a coffee sponge after all, for we shall be having coffee to drink, and it may seem like too much of the same thing. I shall forget about it, let the idea stay in my unconscious mind, and decide tomorrow whether it shall be chocolate or coffee. If it were chocolate I could use real chocolate, plain or dark, melted, or cocoa. Tim has said something about drinks, a liqueur, benedictine, or tia maria, but I am not sure how to time drinks and I don't want to disgrace myself by showing ignorance.

I don't know if I have told you that Terry and Josie cannot come on Saturday because of their children's chicken-pox. We shall have to entertain the Bessicks alone. What a frightening prospect. I am relying on Beethoven's Fifth Symphony to break the ice.

January 25th

I am afraid for tomorrow night.

Sunday

Well, it is over now and I can look at it calmly and with indifference. Shall I describe last night? Well, before they came I had the children put to bed and the baby given her bottle, and the sitting room arranged cosily and, I hope, tastefully, with the chairs and couches (our furniture is Swedish make) placed at what Tim and I consider the correct angle so as to make conversation easier and more intimate. I dusted the radiogram and blew the fluff from the long-playing needle, and left the Fifth Symphony lying upon the cabinet. I could not help leaving a few of our more intellectual books lying around, carelessly, as if we used them every day, some of them half-open, or open at pages of difficult words; also a collection of Van Gogh prints, and an isolated Picasso, which I propped up on the top shelf of the bookcase. It was one of Picasso's that I cannot make head or tail of, yet it gives a certain impression and surely no visitor, I thought, would be boorish enough to ask me to explain the meaning of it.

Tim had decided that we wouldn't have any drinks, only coffee, and that the cake had better be choclate, with walnuts, for variety. I prepared to make a number of narrow slices of toast with a sardine, or a slice of tomato, lying upon each. Above all I wanted our evening to be a *natural* one, with none of the artificialities one finds—everyone at ease and happy.

They came at eight o'clock. I was aflutter when I heard their car—one of the latest, with engine in the back. I dashed to the bathroom for a final powdering and a new touch of lipstick and whipped open the cupboard door to make sure the plates and coffee cups were ready, and as a last minute thought, I put the Picasso, face downward, upon the card table. I was afraid suddenly that Dr Herbert would say, outright—What is your interpretation of this picture, Mrs Harlow? (Later, I thought, when we become friends, we shall of course be Tim and Teresa and Herbert and Alison). Then I answered the knock at the door, quite coolly, though my voice shook, and I was forced to clear my throat.

They are such nice people. We were Tim and Teresa and Herbert and Alison right from the very first, though I do not remember actually addressing the doctor by his christian name in case it sounded familiar, though he has travelled overseas and does not worry about such things. He called me Teresa. His voice is very soft, almost like fur, and he is dark, slightly bald, with brown eyes, almost black at times; and his wife is the opposite, very thin, with fair hair and large grey eyes, nondescript except for their size. She has a protruding upper lip, something to do with her teeth, which gives her a horsey expression. Admittedly she is good-looking in other ways, her eyes for example, but I can see what Josie means when she describes her as a shrew. The expression is latent. She kept referring to her husband as *Doctor*. I could see she is conceited about being a doctor's wife. Yet I enjoyed the evening. We played the Fifth Symphony, and Herbert said, instantly— Fate knocks on the door.

And he (Herbert I mean, not Fate) gave me quite a special sort of smile. Herbert (forgive me if it sounds familiar) tapped with his hand upon the side of the chair and nodded his head to the music, with an understanding look in his eye, while his wife sat with a slight smile on her face and her eyes in a kind of dream which I must confess made them rather ethereal. I had prepared to nod my head and tap too, to show my familiarity with the piece, but I had to devise some other means of keeping time. I swayed backward and forward with, I hope, an intelligent expression on my face. Tim said afterwards that I looked like a charmed snake. Dear Tim, what a tease he is!

After the music Dr Bessick (I have decided that the name Herbert sounds too familiar) exclaimed that the Fifth Symphony was one of his first loves, and repeated the words— Fate knocks at the door, again glancing at me with a special look in his eye.

He said something in French then, which, although I thought rapidly to connect with any sentences of French words I knew, I could not understand, and answered—Yes, yes, rather foolishly, but with French gestures, for compensation. I did hope then to make a remark in French to show him that I knew a little of the language, but alas all I could think of was—*Le chat court vite. Le rat court vite aussi.*

Oh, we had the usual annoying things happen in the evening. The sardines came out squashed, and I burned a couple of slices of toast. They complimented me on the coffee. They said—Do you grind your own coffee?

I was about to say, of course not, when I realized that it is apparently the thing to grind your own coffee, so I said— I have been thinking of doing so.

Oh, you find the bought coffee ghastly too, questioned Mrs Bessick.

I told her I found the bought coffee hopeless, but managed to process it in some way.

Oh, we talked then about capital punishment and the Far East, and the psychology of the child, and Alison told me of her child, Magdalen, very highly strung and delicate and brilliant—Poor little Magdalen, I said. She will suffer.

And Alison said—It's terrible. We don't know what kind of world our children will grow up into. If only something could be done about the state of the world.

We were both silent then, and depressed. I agreed—If only something could be done about the state of the world.

The Bessicks have promised to come again, or ring us quite soon. I believe now, fingers crossed, that we are established in the right society.

Thursday, February the something

Everything is flat. The Bessicks have not rung, and thinking it over, I believe they never will. The weather continues hot and at night the air breathes mosquitoes. I cannot remember a summer for so long without rain. The ground is like a baked brick, cracked and hard, and the children dance over the cracks and call them earthquakes. Of late in the afternoon I have been taking a rug on the lawn and lying down in my sun-suit, lazily drowsing or looking up at the sky where you can see the waves of heat moving and shimmering. I remember when we were children we used to lie for hours looking up at the sky in autumn when the thistledown sailed above the cloud, sailed or scurried on an urgent voyaging. Where? And then a cloud would cross the sun and we would shiver for the blocked warmth, and it would seem as if there had never been any sun, as if we had lived always in cold; until the cloud passed and we shivered for the warmth of new sun upon our backs, between the shoulder-blades where cold and hot strike. It's funny, the sky up in the north here is different from the sky in the south, and the light too. Down in the south you feel all the time a kind of formidable background, like a block of grey shadow, of a continent of ice, Antarctica in the wings. The dark there is more frightening and less friendly, you are trapped in it as in a tomb, and the stone of ice will not roll away. Up here at night there is a kind of upper daylight, high in the sky, as if the dark were clinging closer to the earth under the whip and strike of sun. But, why, how strangely I express myself. I was thinking of the letter Daphne wrote to me, about dark and light and a continent of ice. I must send her a tin of biscuits.

By the way I had a letter from my mother to say that Toby is coming north for a night and expects to stay with me. I don't want him to come. He lazes around and expects to have everything done for him, and he won't eat this and he won't eat that, like a spoilt child, the way he acts at home. And I'm afraid he would disgrace me and take a fit when I had visitors. I shall live in terror that some of my friends will call and see Toby hanging around with his dirty fingernails and greasy hair. Perhaps I should be sorry for him. But his life is so apart from mine, him poking about in these rubbish dumps for scrap iron and bottles and things to sell, almost as if he were still a child. He goes back and back to the rubbish dumps as a child goes to a wound, tearing the plaster off so that it never heals but festers always. I do not know why I thought of that. I just thought of it.

February 11th. Monday

The Bessicks have still not rung, as they promised. Rain today and I could have put my tongue out and drunk it straight from the sky. It was the kind of rain that smokes with warmth. If I were in the south now there would be signs of autumn, leaves turning, and the chill in the late afternoon, and the beginning of mushrooms in the sheltered and more dewy places. Here there seems nothing but warmth and everlasting summer. I had another letter from Daphne, a very strange letter. I don't know if they will ever cure her, even with these modern treatments like electric shock and insulin shock and that new kind of brain operation you read about in the papers, the kind where they change the personality. How terrible to be deprived of one's personality.

February 18th. Monday

Alison Bessick has been shot through the left lung and they have arrested her husband for murder. Isn't it awful? I can scarcely believe it. In spite of the fact that it is in this morning's paper, on the middle page, with a photo of their house and the room where the murder was committed. I can scarcely believe it. Isn't it awful, really awful?

February 19th. Tuesday

The place is agog with the Bessick murder. There are all

kinds of rumours. Some say she was carrying on with a man from one of the East Coast bays, some say *he* was carrying on with one of his women patients, and that Alison found out and confronted him and he shot her, in cold blood. Some say he went berserk and that his counsel will put in a plea for not guilty on the grounds on insanity. Others say his wife had it coming to her. You've no idea, there are so many rumours. Our home was one of the last they visited together. To think of it. I see now when I look back on our evening that things were not as they should have been between them. He seemed to have a calculating coldness in his manner. I realize the significance of it now.

MARRIED TO A MONSTER. That's the title of one of the films in town this week, and I do believe it applies to some homes where women are forced to suffer cruelty and coldness from their husbands. I thank heaven that Tim is beyond reproach.
February 20th. Wednesday

I have heard that Dr Bessick made no denial of the fact of murdering his wife. He had planned it, he said, for months, and was happy to have his plans carried out. His wife had been inconsiderate and wayward, spending a large part of the housekeeping money on make-up and perfume and hats, and failing to provide satisfying meals, and instead, opened tinned food for every meal. They say all this. But I do feel sorry for Herbert. I cannot help remembering the night he spoke so kindly to me, as if we had known each other for years. I only wish I had thought of some French sentence that night.
Thursday

The fuss about the murder has almost died down. Tim and I have gained much prestige from being some of the last to have the Bessicks visit. Another doctor and his wife, the Broadfoots, have asked us to their home next week, and though I cannot go this time, it is the knowing that we have been asked that gives a happy feeling. What more can one ask of life than to be popular and sought after.
February 23rd. Saturday

This afternoon we went to the beach in the car. The children spent the time, as children will, making castles of sand and finding shells and listening to the sea singing inside the shell; and paddling. I put Sharon on the edge of the water where the baby waves come in and she tiptoed upon the sand and tried to take the bits of foam in her fingers to put in her mouth. Poor little Sharon. She couldn't understand what had happened when the foam melted away and she found herself holding nothing. I gave her one of the boy's spades to play with then, and she sat beside us on the rug, banging away with her spade and cooing and blowing bubbles. I believe she is almost ready to walk for she sneaks along with one hand to steady her, and is quite surprisingly agile, more so than the boys were at the same age, though Mark walked very early— I think it seems to be that way with your first. Anyway, they are all tucked up in bed, sweet and kissed now, and Tim is listening to the radio. He has just finished working out his sales account.

Sunday

I broke off my diary suddenly last night to sit with Tim and hear the radio. What a peaceful world and how fortunate I am to be so loved and safe. I have found a novel, *The Asses Skin*, by a Frenchman called Balzac. I am not sure whether I shall like it but I met Mrs Dr Broadfoot in town and she recommended the book to me, and I could not refuse to read it. I have read the first three pages. While I remember, I must say that I sneaked into the film MARRIED TO A MONSTER last week, and thought it rather obscene in places. I did not mention to Mrs Dr Broadfoot that I had been in case it was not the kind of film one goes to, even though it was French; but since then I have found out that all the intellectuals are going, and I wish I had mentioned the film to Mrs Broadfoot, it would have compensated for my not having heard of Balzac's *The Skin of the Wild Ass*. But it is too late now for such regrets.

February 25th. Monday

An awful morning in town. I bought a pair of shoes at a sale, and when I came home I found they hurt over the right instep, and I cannot change them. Oh how I hate some of these simpering saleswomen.

A letter from my mother today, the same old story of everything well and faith prevailing. Oh I hate her and wish she would put an end to all suspense and die. She seems to have been ill for long enough. She tells me Dad has been to the hospital to see the doctor about Daphne. He could not see Daphne herself, as apparently she seemed not well enough for visitors. He says the grounds are full of flowers with wide lawns and neatly kept paths, so that the place seems a paradise for the poor deranged folk. No doubt they are happier there than in the outside world. But how shall I face people if they find out I have a sister in an asylum? I am amazed that my father dared to visit there, he is usually so reluctant to make definite journeys or transactions. He is trying to give up smoking. He is afraid of cancer.

March 11th. Monday

Tim has been teasing me about my beauty aids and says—Why don't I write a list of them in my diary. So I have accepted the challenge and shall write some account of my powderings and primpings. I could write a page describing my make-up, my night creams and astringent lotions and my powder bases (I use liquid foundation—I have lately changed over to Wisteria Peach Bloom) my lipstick (Grenadier Red is my favourite, also Poppy and Crimson Flame) my face powder (I have lately gone off the cake make-up for it clogs the pores) my hair shampoo (what a prettily shaped bottle it is in—you really pay for the bottle). Oh, and my talcum powder, perfume, bath oil, deodorant, and that awful stuff I used to take the hair from my underarm and the slight shadow from my top lip. I believe my depilatory is made from lime, intended to burn away the hair, and it has frightening directions on the packet, with large letters,

KEEP AWAY FROM THE EYES.

That frightens me, I am always afraid I shall go blind. How terrible to be blind.

Well you see I have used nearly a page to describe my beauty aids and Tim is laughing at me. Dear Tim! We may be going south sooner than I thought.

I cannot very well refuse to go. But Waimaru! The dead town where nobody smiles and old women talk about you if you wear a suntop or a two-piece bathing-suit. They will, I imagine, treat me like a prodigal daughter returned, as if I had no social standing or dignity, remembering me only as a child who lived in the town and went to school there. And they will pat my children on the head and moon over them, seeing resemblances to myself that I cannot see, which will make me feel baffled and incompetent. And if my father visits us he will shout at the children the way he shouted at us. He will be possessive and address Mark, if he makes a request of the boy—Spring to it, quick and lively, my lad.

He will cuff them over the ears and tell them to be seen and not heard, and muddle up the whole of my child psychology. And my mother will interfere, making up to the children and giving them sweets when she knows they shouldn't have them, bestowing presents and telling stories— Once upon a time—

—Once upon a time, do you know what happened, once upon a time? —No-o-o-o. —Well, it is a story and I shall tell it to you.

My mother will grow young again and be happy, imagining that my children are her own, and being for them the hundred-year-old treasure of wisdom and fairy that children call a grandmother.

And will my father have a supply of sweets to pop in his grandsons' mouths?

This is all a dream and will not be so. My father is irritable and nervous, my mother faded and near death. Oh I long suddenly for my old black-haired grandmother, the one we dreamed of as a negress; who sat like a volcano in a long black dress among the corn and taters of Virginny; my grandmother wise and frizzled in the sun so that her skin smelt of cooking and I climbed on her knee and dug my nose and mouth, like a cannibal, into her steaming flesh.

I must not dream thus. I dread going to Waimaru. The world of childhood widens with every wish of the child that it may be worn like a magic cloak about the shoulder. I shall return to Waimaru and find it, like the skin of the wild ass, shrivelling at my every desire, a shrunken scrap of wrinkle between my thumb and forefinger.

And then—Toby and the rubbish dump where our house has been built. I dare not think of these things.

Morning

I told my fears to Tim last night in bed. He is an angel, smoothing everything so that in the daylight it all seems like nonsense that I wrote last night in my diary. It is not like me to be so unpractical, but sometimes the mood just overtakes me. Tim is an angel, except that he spilt his tea over the clean sheet.

I think autumn will never happen now. Peter tells me he thinks the world has stopped at summer. I think that is true. It will perhaps be summer now for ever.

March 18th. Monday

The Bessick trial began today, and one of the witnesses, of

all people, is the electric light man who came to read the meter. It appears that he overheard Bessick threaten his wife. And a neighbour who found their daughter's kitten that had strayed, heard Alison talking to her husband and saying— This will end soon.

Obviously referring to the situation between them. How terrible. Another terrible thing happened today. Peter and Mark emptied paint from an old tin they had brought inside, upon the sitting room carpet, in the middle of it, too. I don't know how I shall get the stains out unless I write to one of the radio stations or one of the women's magazines. I do try to keep the house tidy. Sharon, though she is ready now for her rocking horse, cannot use it upstairs here because of the damage it will do to the carpet and linoleum. Tim is inclined to think I am too houseproud. Oh, I am tired and unhappy, and I wish something would happen. The grocer overcharged me today for the tea and biscuits. He gave me the biscuits and tea separately, one pound of each, and then charged me for two pounds of both, and tea and chocolate wafers are dear enough as it is.

Two months later

Herbert Bessick was hanged last Friday, in spite of letters to the paper and a petition to the Governor-General for a reprieve. An aunt in England has taken their little Magdalen, poor child with her ballet lessons and her dreams of *Giselle*. The Public Trust has put the Bessick's house for auction. It is a cold situation but has a harbour view so perhaps some wealthy couple will buy it. The furnishings are being sold separately. Josie said they had a cocktail cabinet which she is trying to get at a reduced price if she can. It seems they had a tape recorder too, and a radiogram, specially imported, and a connoisseur's collection of records, obscure quartets and concertos and octets. How they must have laughed when I played the Fifth Symphony, Fate knocking on the door. We shall have to buy something more obscure and difficult for when the Broadfoots come. I shall buy a cheap edition of what to listen to in music, where I shall find enough ideas to keep me stocked for the evening, and I shall remember to look bored and languid if talk changes to the well-known works of the masters.

I was surprised to hear that some of the furniture from the

Bessick's house was quite makeshift and cheap, something I cannot understand, unless they liked it that way, primitive and artistic; but that style is going out now, Josie tells me, and no one socially or artistically high-up would be such a fool as to buy these straw mats and seats that look as if they were taken from the hut of a native chief.

Do you know, I have come to the conclusion that I am a snob. I don't like to think of myself as a snob, yet I seem to be one, though perhaps I'm not, after all, it is just my tenacious honesty that suggests the idea to me. Toby is coming up next month for sure. It will be freezing cold and wild weather and he will walk in like some kind of battered and invalid ghost to warm himself at my space-heater. I think he will stay just one night. I hope that he will stay only one night.

It was Friday morning that Bessick was hanged, early, at the same time that I was crushing the Weetbix on the boys' plates, and sprinkling the sugar, and adding milk; and warming Sharon's bottle. Dear child, she rocks everywhere now, and though Tim keeps telling me to bring the rocking horse up from the garage I find I have to refuse, for the carpets and linoleum will be ruined. Oh, and she crawls around with objects in her mouth, like a puppy. Dear Sharon. I would do anything in the world for the child!

We are not having any more children. Later, we shall send Peter and Mark and Sharon to boarding school, and make plans for going overseas. Tim and I shall join one of the world tours which plan your holiday for you and show you the places that really matter. Oh I love being alive, and when I think of our tour overseas I know that is what I always longed for—luxury and clothes and travel—even when I was a dirty, ragged school child standing in the cold by the school wall, watching the others play skipping,

> All in together
> this fine weather,

and waiting for them to choose me to join in. Sharon will have none of that. I shall buy her, as soon as she is old enough, a skipping rope with painted handles, and a doll's pram with silken tassels hanging from the hood; and a sleeping doll, a walkie-talkie that cries and walks and wets, lying on a satin mattress, her head on an embroidered and frilly pillow case; and a doll's house, and a teaset of real china. I shall buy Sharon everything her heart may desire.

Friday

I still have in my head the terrible dream of last night which caused me to wake up in fear, crying, until Tim made me believe it was not real.

It's only a dream, dear—he kept saying—You had something for tea or supper which disagreed with you.

And I kept saying—It's not a dream, it's real, I know it's real.

How stupid of me. I think now it was those salt crackers and cheese that we had when the Broadfoots came last night, and all the worry of getting ready for them, and thinking what to wear, and trying to remember what books I had read lately and what music I had been listening to.

But my dream, that made me cry in the night, let me tell it.

It happened that Tim and I were preparing in the middle of a desert for a party to be given to two people. I remember the scene well; everywhere lay sand and rotted trees and clumps of withered bushes, and the sun was as hot as if it shone through glass. No river flowed through the waste, nor were there any pools that you might imagine in a desert, with date palms and fringe of green beside the clear water. Nor were there any other people save one, a shrivelled child, an Arab girl, with a white garment wrapped about her, sitting so still she may have been dead, upon a grotesque rocking-horse which rose out of the sand and was painted black with its tongue a bright red and yellow and blue, striped three times.

I have said that Tim and I were preparing to entertain these two unknown people; but we had no food to offer them, nor drink, we simply sat cross-legged upon the sand.

You shall sing for them—Tim said to me—if you can find a song.

And I replied to him—You shall dance for them.

And although I knew there was no food or music I kept staring about me for the coffee and sardines and the radiogram with its Fifth Symphony ready to be played.

And then suddenly the Arab child began to rock upon her rocking-horse, disturbing the sand and dust until they rose in clouds and I saw the sand was grains of gold and the dust too, and I cried out to Tim—Tim, Tim, make her stop it, make her stop it, she is destroying the gold. Look. All those grains will fly up in the sky and we shall never see them again. Make her stop it, Tim.

And Tim answered—But Teresa, she likes it. Look, her little Arab face is covered with smiles. Let her keep rocking.

And I cried back—But the gold, Tim. The gold. Stop her.

So Tim went up to the little girl and spoke to her whereupon she climbed from the horse and both horse and child vanished leaving no trace but the red and yellow and blue tongue, striped three times, grown larger now, and spread out like a carpet upon the sand. Then appeared our two guests, walking upon the carpet. At first I thought they were Alison and Herbert Bessick, indeed they *were* Alison and Herbert Bessick; but as they grew closer I saw they were Tim and me, but different; for Tim was smiling cruelly, and I was holding my hand over my side, under my breast, and it is amazing that I was able to walk, for blood flowed from a wound in my side, and fell, as if in a predisposed pattern, upon the red stripe of the carpet. And so the two dream people approached us, and I began to cry, and turned to Tim for help; but he was not there, I could not see him anywhere, only the two dream-people advancing; and I began to sing, a child's song we had at school, years ago, about Miska and Panni,

Miska came riding by gay was he
Panni stood by the stream fair was she
red his coat yellow boots none so gay
but the stream stood between Panni and her love's way.

And after I had sung the song, the world grew dark suddenly, as I remembered from my geography that it grows dark in the desert, like a cutting off of the sun's life; and I saw, far away and not able to reach it, our house, I could see the louvre windows and cantilever terrace, every detail to the yellow eaves, yet the house seemed made of paper for the walls flapped and fluttered. Now I think of it they were black walls, for I watched them flapping backward and forward for many seconds before I realised I was watching something else flapping. It was a black paper man dangling from the sky.

—Dr Bessick, I cried out.

Then I saw it was Tim, and he held under his arm a portfolio with gold writing on it, I could read it from where I stood, and it said—Sales Account Sales Account Sales Account.

I thought this very funny and began to laugh and then I felt my side hurting and could stand up no longer so I lay down upon the carpet spread in the desert, thinking, I shall die now. Where are Toby and Francie and Daphne? And my mother and father? Francie, Francie, I called out. Toby, Toby. Daphne.

Nobody came. I felt a sense of desolation and unhappiness that nobody came to me. The little Arab girl had appeared again, but was changed and happy, standing smiling and holding a feather of toi-toi in one hand, and a salt cracker, spread with cheese, in the other. I do not think she saw me. I began to cry again, and that was when I woke up and saw in my half-dream state, the black paper man lying dead beside me; and I cried out, it was all so strange, and for one second apart from all the other time, I wanted to be a little girl with dark hair and a dirty spotted pinafore, sitting in the rubbish dump and looking up at the clouds like white slippers or silk fish in the sky.

Now telling that dream has exhausted me. Goodnight.

Saturday

I think there will be a certain delight in returning to Waimaru—in revealing to the people who knew me as a child and have me in their memory as a ragged little dark girl, a *chicken*, a quiet shy high-school girl with a tunic so small it could not cope with my even so slight development; a draggled-looking outcast going messages to the butcher's or grocer's or papershop, and saying, afraid, for I had no money warm in my hand—Sixpenceworth the mince, please, or—Two pounds of skirt steak and twopenceworth the mince for the cat; will there not be a crowing delight when I return and people realise that I am grown-up and married, with children (two boys and a girl—where would any distribution be found more favourable?), that my home contains a washing machine, an electrolux, a refrigerator, a steam iron, an electric range, and all the modern devices that my mother never dreamed of, and that half my former friends, I am sure, will never have. Oh, stuck in Waimaru, how shall I bear it, if it were not for what I have to *show*?

Wednesday

News this morning that mother has died. The telegram said she passed away peacefully in the night, and that all is well. How strange to have written all is well! It almost seems like a postscript delivered by my mother herself. *Is* she dead? I have not cried yet, it all seems so far away. We are not going south for the funeral, it is impossible with the children and everything, but we have sent a beautiful wreath of earliest violets and narcissus and a card brought from Petersons, who specialise in tasteful printing for funerals, weddings, birthdays, and other important occasions.

But what will mother look like? Will she look like parchment and her eyelids hang like yellow crepe, as I have read in a book? I do not really believe she is dead, yet I am glad, I am glad of her death.

Thursday

Have received a few telegrams and cards of sympathy from friends who know about mother, or read it in the papers. I wish Dad had not put—

I go to prepare a place for you,

or some other text in the paper—it seems so lacking in taste; and now I suppose every year the family will think of some rhyme to publish in the memorial column, and disgrace me in front of my artistic friends.

The funeral today.

Peter had a letter from the school nurse to say his teeth needed attention, and will I take him to the clinic next Tuesday at three o'clock.

Mother will be buried in the family grave if there is room for her. But my father will languish, I fear he will die, and how strange with my father dead, the little hopping man of cruelty, tyranny, and child-like dependence. What will Toby do? And Daphne?

Oh my mother was as big as the arm of land will hold sea and not spill. I cannot imagine her death. I think of her at home putting the pikelets on the girdle or singing her kind of half-song as she wiped the dishes with the end of a dirty and wet tea-towel, or standing in the snow when we lived in the deep south in the railway huts red like geraniums; with her boots bogged in the white, standing and saying to us, —Kiddies, kiddies a little waxeye has come to us in the cold weather, and meaning, Kiddies, a waxeye had come to her to hide from the snow and find honey in her, for she knew her bigness and sweetness and could not move for spilling some of it, though I would have held my arms, like land around a lake, tight about her, and not let her spill over for anyone save myself, for I was youngest; and yet it is not my mother I grieve for, it is herself as grandmother for my children; only, yes, it is my mother too, who should have died long ago she was so tired with sweeping out her house and the world;

and I used to climb on her knee and pull open her blouse,
and take her tittie in my mouth, for there was no one who
came after me, to say
—It's mine.

Oh, I don't know, I am half Daphne in writing this, it is
not my usual way; as if a spell had come over me.

Friday

Back to normal. I seem to have lost count of the date. Toby
is coming next week for a night. I have prayed and prayed
that he will not come, for we are friends now with the Broadfoots, and if Harold, that is Dr Broadfoot, sees Toby and
perhaps guesses that he takes fits—it is manifest from Toby's
eyes and his flushed face and his occasional stumbling in
speech, almost a drunken slur—if Harold notices it all, I shall
never recover from the disgrace. Toby, why do you not see
that I don't want you, that you have no part in my life, that
I, who played with you as a little girl, finding treasure and
curious wonders in the rubbish dump, am a grown woman
living a happy normal life, and want nothing, ever, to do with
your strange ways and your falling down in fits.

29

Toby did not read any more of the diary. He
closed the book and leaned forward and thrust it upon the fire;
then, remembering that he had seen in the garage underneath
the house a wooden rocking-horse, he crept outside and down
the stairs, turning the light on in the garage, and looking at the
bright blue rocking-horse with its gold stirrups and silver bit,
everlasting in the wooden mouth, and the marble eyes that
blinked once, twice, in the light; and Toby picked up the
rocking-horse and holding it before him, he climbed the stairs
and carried the bright blue toy into the middle of the sitting-
room where it stood upon the green-leaved carpet like a living
horse in a warm forest. Then Toby went to Sharon's room.
The child lay uncovered and flushed in her cot, her hand upon
a half-empty bottle of milk which she drew, in her sleep,
towards her, sucking, and wriggling her toes with the pleasure
of her dream-tasting. Toby lifted her and she began to cry.
He covered her with a blanket from the cot and carried her
to the sitting-room where he put her in the saddle of the
rocking-horse, closing her fists upon the reins.

—Rock, he said gently.

And he chucked her under the chin and said,

—Oogle, oogle, oogle,

the way his own uncles had done, or his imagining of their way, when he was a child, but a tiny starveling with no rocking-horse.

—Rock. Go on, rock.

The child seemed not to understand, and kept crying, and Toby leaned forward, rocking the horse but the child did not stop crying, softly now, and dribbling over her fat chin; so he took her, his dirty and hairy hands encircling her warm silk body, and sat by the fire. The diary was almost burned now, he felt no guilt that he had burned it. The flames liked their food and poked, like a row of vindictive eyes, through the half-drooped glass eyelids of the space-heater.

—Now, have you had enough warm? Toby asked his eleven-month-old niece who could not, because of drowsiness and the silence that babies have, say one word in answer, but slept now in his arms.

He carried her back to the cot, covered her, tucking her tight; and returning to the now empty and damp forest, treading upon the dead and dying leaves, he replaced the amazed and blinking horse downstairs in the garage. There was a frost upon the grass, shining like dibbles of white soup upon a green beard, and Toby's breath as he climbed the stairs, came out like smoke from the mouth of no dragon, only from Toby Withers, numbed cold and not knowing where.

And then he took his folding suitcase that sank, when empty, like a concertina; that had belonged to Uncle Louis who died of cancer in the small upstairs room of lanoline and yellow skin and the smell, in early spring when he died, of raspberry cordial flowing through the air coloured blue and too sweet for tasting, put in his pyjamas, hairbrush, brilliantine, soap, el ctric shaver, jersey; snapped shut the worn empty-of-music suitcase and left his sister's house, and crossed by the ferry to the city they called a jungle.

And he felt tired and his mother said goodbye to him from the platform, taking out her lace handkerchief, the only one left from the first war, when Bob sent them from Paris— *Toujours L'amour* embroidered across the corner; to wave goodbye, Toby; and tell, with the aid of a waving handkerchief,

what to remember and do on such a long voyage from home
to a strange city of trams and traffic lights and trolley buses
and gangsters—yes gangsters walking in broad daylight, with
guns in their hip pockets; and masks of black silk ready.

—Goodbye, Toby.

And then what to remember,

—Remember the train goes right through to the boat. Don't
get off at Christchurch.

—Remember not to put your head out of the window when
you're travelling, or it will be sliced off, and roll down
between the rails and be mangled, Toby. Mangled.

A man was mangled last week, leaving a wife and three
children.

—Remember, Toby. When you get on the boat ask politely
the way to your cabin if you get lost; then go to bed; eat a
water biscuit; and go with the motion of the boat.

—Also, don't put your head out of the porthole.

—Aunty and Uncle will be there to meet you in Wellington
and they will take you to the train at night. Take your
pills, Toby, and be good. And never never speak to
strangers, and if a nice man offers you a bag of lollies or
an ice-cream, say No thank you.

So she said goodbye and kept waving her lace hanky in
case Toby looked back to see, but he didn't look because that
would have meant putting his head out of the window and
having it sliced off, and travelling the rest of the way with
no head. He sat watching the steam rise to the outside of the
carriage windows, and through the steam he peered at the
leafless and sodden paddocks with their broken-down fences
and tottering half-hinged gates; at the patches of swamp and
flax; the lidded haystacks; a few sheep, early-shorn, looking
woe-begone, their wool peeled and whittled; and white as
coconut; and three magpies flew up from near the train and
Toby, seeing their evil beaks, knew that magpies pick the eyes
out of children, even through carriage windows; so he thought,

—I'll hide in the lavatory until the magpies pass.

So he went down the aisle, saying excuse me whenever he
bumped into anyone, and, opening the carriage door, was
almost whirled away with the roar of going; and he felt afraid
and opened the door which said—Gentlemen's Toilet.

And he looked down at the lavatory and watched the ground
rushing past, the gravel and bits of green that would mean

dock or dandelion; and he thought, wondering, It will drop all along the railway lines, in the middle, and men will come with shovels and shovel it up. Next time I shall look on the railway line and find out for myself. We will all look. What will Francie be doing now, and Chicks and Daphne? Oh, Oh, what if they find my very secret alone hut in the pine trees!

After he had finished he had a drink of water out of a paper cup that he folded to make, and he threw that down to watch it drop. And then he thought The magpies will be gone; and opened the door into the rush and thunder of go-it go-it go-it de-light-ed-ly de-light-ed-ly the Lim-it-ed; and found his way to his seat in the corner; again saying excuse me to anyone he bumped into, though not smiling because they were strangers and criminals with bags of lollies in their pockets, to offer him before they carried out their plans of kidnapping.

And sometimes as he sat watching the world travel, and the rivers, and bridges, he remembered his mother waving good-bye to him and telling him the list of not-tos, and he thought, What if I am going away and will never see her again? What if this is really a way of selling me, by sending me for a holiday in the northern city, to be taken away on a foreign boat. And he remembered the boats he had seen sometimes on the wharves, the red and yellow and white boats, with flags flying; and water coming in a rude way out of the sides of the boats; and the sea nudging the sides; and men walking about with telescopes in their hands, and crying out Heave-ho, Heave-ho.

But that thought was just to tease him for he knew his mother would be waiting when he came back, and his sisters too, and they would say—Did you have any fits?

And he knew that Mrs Robinson over the road would ask after him for he remembered her saying,

—Fancy Mrs Withers letting her boy go for a holiday by himself, him with his fits.

They met him in Wellington, Uncle and Aunty. They took him on a train where the doors shut without being touched, as if they were told to; to their house where Uncle said the surrounding hills were

—Second growth bush, my boy.

There was a dead tree in the backyard and a rope clothes-line and a garage with a tin roof; and everywhere you looked from the backyard you saw houses and people's washing and coal-boxes through the fence; and you heard people speaking to each other and people coughing; and the air above the house was empty and cold, with no traffic of birds. And Toby's cousin played the organ, the boy cousin, and was religious, with hymns, and the girl cousin said grace at the table, with no warning, so that Toby had begun to eat, and his uncle frowned at him. And they took him for the day to the Gardens first, through the hothouse, treading over the hoses and touching giant pink flowers that were labelled in foreign language on a piece of wood, tied up, so they could not escape; and every flower in the hothouse and fern in the fernery was there to be looked at, and what a crowd of people walking up and down and looking, turning their heads and saying,

—That's a lovely colour,

or

—I like that shade, it's like Mag's dress, only deeper,

or

—You can get that colour now, in that stuff you don't have to iron,

or

—What lovely flowers! They just make you realise, don't they?

All the people turning their heads backwards and forwards like dolls.

So Toby spent the day looking, next at the Sound Shell, where bands played, and then at the Zoo where the polar bear wore an old yellow fur coat, and his eyes were runny and red as if he had a cold. All the animals seemed to have sore eyes as if they had been looking too much in the daylight, and Toby wondered if perhaps his aunt and uncle and his two cousins and himself had red eyes with all their looking, and he said to his cousin,

—Are my eyes red?

—Don't be silly, she said. Your eyes are only red when you've been crying or something like that.

And then Uncle, who was interested in history, took them to watch the tuatara. They stood half an hour waiting for it to move, but it seemed to be asleep, and the house where it lived was stuffy, and the girl cousin wanted to go to the lavatory, and so did everybody but nobody had liked to say.

So they went down under the monument, the women in the women's side and Toby and his boy cousin and his uncle in the men's side. The floor was stone and covered with a slimy green moss. There was a tap that kept dripping and could not be turned off. And there was a small window that couldn't be seen through; it was broken and patched with wire-netting, and Uncle said it had been smashed by juvenile delinquents, there were many of them, he said, in the city.

Toby asked what they looked like, and what language they spoke, and if they dressed like people, and did they live in burrows or what. And Uncle said, with the same voice he had used for saying,

—Second-growth bush, my boy.

—You are ignorant as yet, Toby. The city is a terrible place.

30

So he walked all night, carrying his suitcase and overcoat, up and down the streets of the city they called a jungle. At first when he arrived there he saw few people—a policeman walking along trying the door-handles of shops; motor-cyclists with leather jackets and goggles, crowded outside a milk-bar; a woman, Chicks, tall and dark and pale with the colour washed from her face and her eyes tired, standing outside the Post Office in front of the letterboxes with their obscene and magnified mouths. And Toby thought of the story about the soul flying from the body, and then, from everyone who passed he watched their soul fly out and into the letterbox, and them walk away spiritless and unknowing. And he saw a little boy who looked up at him fearfully, thinking,

That man has a bag of lollies in his pocket for me, and a mask made of black silk, and a ray gun, and a space-ship parked quite close, invisible, ready to kidnap me to the moon or Mars. And the child backed, terrified, when Toby addressed him,

—Hello, little man, are you lost?

Then it was the dead and wet and street-shining time before the pictures finished, and there was a tall man wearing a black silk coat as wet and shining as the street, and he was walking from nowhere to nowhere. He was a hotel night porter on his way to work, to spread out his newspapers in the hotel pantry, and empty the shoe polish and brushes from the box onto the paper, and carry the shoes from outside the doors, remembering which, to be polished, with his pale immune hand hid for two or three half-minutes within each bulged and empty nest of leather; to climb inside the lift, then, with the gates shutting their iron teeth behind him; and sit in the safe shut box, on a wooden stool, to wait and be rung for, all night, till the boiling of the first egg in the morning for the early breakfasts, and the flipping under the door of the first newspaper; and the cook arriving for duty and peeling up her sleeve and saying

—I have red elbows. Look, I have red elbows.

All evening Toby walked the streets. And the people of the city who had been held inside theatres and halls by some kind of elastic, corseted there, came flying out, burst and undone, upon the footpath at ten or eleven o'clock; lying down and picking themselves up in one movement so that their falling seemed more of a dream; scurrying then for trams and buses and ferries, the women fatted and furred, with baskets of fruit, cherries or grapes hanging from their ears; the men escorting, rich and prosperous, but not all; nor all of the women with a garden in their face.

Toby watched the same tall and pale woman walk near him, and he said,

—Chicks.

She stopped and said,

—I'd choose a better name if I were you, otherwise nothing doing.

—Teresa, then, said Toby. Only it's just my sister.

—What an exciting relation. Are you waiting for her?

—No. I found her dead and I don't know what to do.

—Call the police or the doctor, and wipe away all fingerprints from your eyes.

—My mother died not long ago.

The girl, Marjorie, thought, Oh what a little country boy with his bag and raincoat, come up to the city from the farm, to see the sights and be shown the places, scared and wanting his mother and sister. She smiled to herself. And I'm the same. Dressed for my part and speaking tough since I worked at the factory.

She thought, I'll have to do the work, and said

—Come for fish and chips, in here, and we can talk.

And she led Toby into the restaurant and they sat at a small table covered with glass, and underneath the glass two paper doilies stained with equal parts of Worcester and tomato sauce. And they ordered fish and chips and coffee for two, and a crimson waitress put before them, after twenty minutes, two narrow slices of bread, two balls of butter printed with a fancy pattern and two plates of fish and chips; also two cups of coffee that looked, Marjorie said, the colour of the Waikato in flood.

And then she said,

—I work in a factory, you know, making stockings. I started off at the woollen mills, and then went to the chocolate factory but it made me fat, so now I'm at stockings. When I've enough nylons for my box I'm going to work at Eudora Underwear.

She leaned forward to Toby, cupping her hand over her mouth to make sure no one else heard her whisper,

—I'm going blind. Can you tell I'm going blind? Next year, or the year after I shall tap with a white stick and make baskets.

And Toby, standing by himself, or walking along the streets, looking in the shopwindows at the radios and washing-machines and carpets and jewels and books and clothes and toys, and the unspeaking lonely shadows of people, saw the girl, Marjorie or Fay or Chicks or whatever had been her name, walking arm in arm with a sailor; and he thought, I wonder. What if I had spoken to her? What if I had spoken to her. He saw them vanish in the dark.

And then he remembered, from his dreaming, that on his return from this holiday in the city, his mother would not be at the station to meet him, to ask if he had taken any fits, and remembered to give his ticket to the guard, and not got out at the wrong station or put his head out of the window, or spoken to strangers; and he was glad he had not spoken to the pale dark girl, for his mother was not long in the grave, she was locked up under the earth, and she could never bear to be locked, even in clothes or cheap beads tight about her neck, and would unbutton the top of her dress and unclasp the beads, more easily to breathe and be free.

31

August the Something

Really, I never seem to know the date since I began my new diary after I lost the old one. I cannot understand what happened to it. Tim teases me and says he has it hidden and reads it and enjoys it; but I know he is merely teasing me. I remember it was after Toby left that I lost it, and Toby left so suddenly, why the children could have been burned to death that night and us been in the *Evening Star* as an example of parents who leave their children alone at night. And I don't know whatever Toby did to the sitting-room carpet, for it is spoiled for always, the mess he made of it.

We go south next month. I cannot contain my excitement, nor can the children, who have asked and asked about the house and I have answered and answered their questions till I am tired.

—Where is it, Mummy?

—Where mummy used to live when she was a little girl.

—But *where*?

—On an old rubbish dump.

(I like to give accurate answers to the children's questions)

—What's a rubbish dump?

—It's the sort of place where all kinds of nasty things are put, that nobody wants.

—Do they put children there?

—No, child. Anyway, it's filled in and you shan't see it.

—You mean it can't come up as a ghost because our house is on top, like putting the cork in a bottle and holding it tight?

Later

I read this page to Tim, and he is amused at the children's questions. Dear Tim.

By the way, I believe they are going to perform some kind of operation on Daphne, to make her normal.

And now I must read a chapter from my book, *Cry, the Beloved Country*, which describes the negro question in South Africa.

32

DAPHNE

There is a place in the south called Arrowtown where the light is frozen pale gold upon a street of poplars whose leaves are pale gold for ever, ready to fall, yet never falling; nor do the trees move; nor the clouds, heliotrope to snow like the berries *acmena flora bunda* from their twig of sky. And the houses there are blurred like smoke shaped from a yellow and blue fire; the people scarved and cloaked with yellow and blue cloud. And if you listen, in that street, you hear nothing, nor do the people there move, nor can you ever walk there unless you break the glass and climb through, bleeding, a crazed myopic figure, to the picture hanging upon the wall of the dayroom where Daphne lives.

The picture is called, ARROWTOWN IN AUTUMN, WITH THE REMARKABLES.

The Remarkables are mountains.

But half-imagined only; with the patients fastening their dream upon the picture and creating beyond the yellow and blue cloud their frozen slope of thought whose blizzard, emerging from the stillness, cut from snow-block of day-after-day dreaming, will blow like swans or arrows flying from the yellow and blue cloud's mouth to whip or sing in the demented night of four walls and the dead bulb of milk behind wire; and the eyes of the world from hour to hour staring through, amazed at the white storm and not knowing why.

And in the morning the pink people come to unlock the door, and struggle through the snow to the frozen bodies that are heaped on little trollies decorated with flags red and white and blue and a beryl stone, and wheeled to the rubbish dump, to be scattered amongst the toi-toi or burned.

33

At first when the world changed its colour and form and Daphne was taken to Arrowtown in autumn, with the Remarkables, there was a woman with grey hair and a coiled face like wire, and sand-stone eyes, who led Daphne from the ambulance in the door to the bathroom where a trough had been scooped from a side of one of the mountains, and luke-warm water poured in.

—You must have a bath, the woman said. Get in.

Her name was Flora Norris, and the wire of her face had been stolen from the wires of wreaths of poppy and nasturtium laid on the grave of her imagined lover, twenty years ago. She was matron of the hospital, Chief of the Remarkables, except for the tribe that wore coats of snow and raided, every morning, the poplar world and the blue and yellow cloud of people. But Daphne did not know of that. She sat in the bath, and rubbed her finger over the sand-stone eyes of the matron. She shivered, and lay down in the trough, and took in her hand a little cake of cream that smelt like washday and the sheets bubbling in the copper.

—Don't eat it. Wash with it, Flora Norris commanded.

Daphne rubbed the cream over her body to soothe the raw skin where the sand-stone had grazed and hurt. And then the woman poured a waterfall from an enema can, over her hair and said

—Now get out and put this nightie on.

But first,

—Any scars? she said. Any operations? Let me look.

She grazed Daphne's body again so that the washing with cream had really been no help, but she did not find the scars the pine needles had sewn; so she pulled something square and striped, with arms out, like an empty scarecrow waiting to be filled, over Daphne's head; and the pink woman who helped her led Daphne to a row of compartments, like horse-boxes, with swinging doors and room to look over and under, and said, sharply

—Do you want to go? Well hurry.

She poked her head over the door while Daphne sat on the seat. And then,

—Ready, said Flora Norris. Use that piece of apple-paper to wipe yourself.

And then,

—Quick now, into bed with you.

And then she smiled and the wire round her face melted and trickled down her neck inside her white uniform so that it tickled or speared, and she thrust her hand down to fetch it and replace it, and undo the smile.

—Remember, she said sternly, everybody is trying to help you. It's up to you to co-operate and pull yourself together.

Daphne lay in bed, nearest the fireplace; with rubber, like a doormat, spread underneath the sheet; and Onward, Onward, written across the bottom of the quilt. And the little old Mother Superior, passing with a basket of linen, towels and sheets and pillowcases for tomorrow; the Irishwoman, with the zipped fur boots and the sea eyes and the black and grey beard, came close to Daphne's pillow and whispered,

—Hello, and why don't you speak?

—Leave her, the nurse said, arranging and counting and marking Daphne's clothes.

—Leave her. This is Daphne. She is too ill to understand what you say.

And Daphne, listening, thought—Oh, what a whopper. There is nothing in the world the matter with me, except that I have been bathed in a trough and dipped under a waterfall and the pine-needles picked from my scars so that they bleed invisible blood. Oh, what a whopper. I will show her immediately that she is wrong.

And she folded back the bedclothes and dangled her foot on the slippery brown mirror that was spread like a floor across the room and, leaping from her bed, she hurried out the door and into the passage. Now where?

But the nurses, touching and folding her clothes in their suitcase, called out

—Get her! Get her!

And five shadows appeared, so that she was put in a little house on the side of the mountain; and she cried to be let out, only to stand on the doorstep and look over at the world and the gentians and the snowgrass or to see if God were saying Blessed are the meek and the poor in spirit.

But the five shadows whispered outside the door, and a sixth crept by, and suddenly they opened the door and seized Daphne and carried her to another house on the side of the mountain; there were many houses, all small and made of snow and iron; but this one was strong, with no light, and a smell of straw, and in the corner a round rubber vessel like a top hat upside-down, or a homberg that a cabinet minister may wear; only it was a chamber, and one of the shadows said,

—Use it, Daphne. We want a specimen.

And all the time outside the sheep were sitting on the lower slopes of the mountain, and the blanket of snow higher up, and ducks rising, like rainbows, from the black pools of the valley.

34

And Daphne lived there alone for many years, amid the assault and insinuation of sound in days unshining and nights without darkness; first the farm cries from the hill, the lariat of surging animal talk whipped in and out of the morning mist; the ear strangled in a noose of bark, crow, cry; and scream from the other farm, the down-place with its row of stables rich with steaming manure from imbeciles and the long-dead mad plotting their daily treasure in the small mountain room of four corners and a wooden pocket window. And the struggle to take hold of time between the slat-shadows of an unreal sun, for there the day is day but never.

And the whistle, the hooter, sounds at some hour like the scream of the mill, and Daphne remembers the poplar mornings and their tall slain shadow with the blood seeping through the coverlet of leaves, and the pearls of ice in the heart of cabbages for kings and queens; and the sticky shine of a snail's track; and the desolate ragged sky, comfortless, like a cheap cotton blanket that would not warm and the wind poked through. And the mill girls going on bicycles, chased by the south wind to their rooms of blindness; but not here, Daphne, here at the hour of the hooter, the door outside the mountain hovel is unlocked, some other door of a brick house holding the idiots and maimed and the dwarves with their crepe faces and parchment eyes, and these people move into the yard; they jabber, jibber and are quiet; they know what you say to them; they know, they are *understanding*, so they must work; and off they skip and limp and crawl, with bundles of soiled clothes under their arm to the laundry; all day with the hiss of steam like snakes in their ears; ironing, folding, hanging out the clothes; feeding and being crushed, their heads and the bones in their heads, under the mangle that is time, taking the sheets of earth they lie between and the pillow-cases of dream they rest their hearts on. They are tired and tireless, their faces are hot, and they roll up the sleeves of their print smocks and sit all together, with their wine and loaves of bread in the centre; and at mid-morning they drink their wine and break their loaves of bread, and are satisfied. And the men tell stories, and walk in the doctor's pyjamas, smiling and shaking hands and bowing because they are Gods in flannelette; but all is not peace; for they quarrel and scream and fight for the last loaf of bread and the last glass of wine till the overseer comes back from her cosy corner, her mouth floured and moist with hot scone; and the hooter sounds once more and the mangles begin their revolutions of pitiless greed; and the wine and bread spill from the jibbering jabbering and quiet mouths, and they die till the midday renewal of the feast, in the brick house on the side of the mountain. Daphne hears them returning shuffling, whimpering, like dogs to their kennel; and then the silence of grace,

     O Lord be blessed for this meat.

The hand of silence over their mouths till the first taste that brings peace and war, while the matron and the ward sister, in white communion with the speech of mill and laundry, flow like waves from table to table, spilling and salt and omnipotent.

After the meal the half-minute to arrange the head and focus the withered eyes back to the heat and steam; the punctual siren demanding, like a sheriff set in the sky the condemned body of imbecile and long-dead mad, the skipping and sweet and blundering procession to the place of the mangle, and the afternoon death and feast, till night without darkness and the new day unshining.

35

And Daphne lived there alone for many years. It is quiet in the mountain room. Will Toby come or Francie or Chicks, or the mother and father who are set like sculpture, in the same place for ever, with their lives growing up through their body like grass through an ageing monument of stone? Who will come, into the quiet?

Someone stirs in the next room, and sings to curse the west wind and all men, and it is Mona with the olive skin and dark hair and brown eyes like darkened beer. She wants her child back to look at and feed and teach to hate, and sing to,

—Like this, she says, with my ukelele or guitar in my hand, now what shall I sing. Ah!

Sunny Australian sweetheart,
I'm in love with you.

—And then the rollicking one, my child, that your father, curse him, sang

I'm a rambler, I'm a gambler, I'm a long way from home
And if you don't like me then leave me alone.
I eat when I'm hungry and I drink when I'm dry,
And if moonshine don't kill me, I'll live till I die.

And then, in case her child that she holds now in her arms to sing to and teach to hate, may be left hungry, she thinks of its food and tells from the side of the mountain to the world, not of milk flowing rich and yellow, crusted with love, from the breast or the cow's teat when the new calf butts and dances, hornless and still wet from birth: but

cheese blisters, how to mix them, how to cook them, and

—Do you know cheese blisters, Mona cries. Do you *know* them? They crackle and are salt, like blood, mixed with cheese that is old soured milk, skim milk, blue and deprived, the dregs of love. Do you know cheese blisters? Do you *know* them? Is there anyone there to answer me?

Daphne, in the next room, does not answer, for she waits for Toby to come, or Francie, or Chicks with a little pocket of wheat to share and share alike. Ah, there is a footstep outside the door, the eyes of the world look through the hole in the door, the key turns in the lock and here is a member of the white tribe, the chief perhaps, come to say why and where and how.

And then,

—Now. Where are you? the chief said. Do you know now where you are? You have been sick for a long time. What month and year is it? Or what day? Do you know your name?

And then,

—Why are you here? Do you know why you are here?

And all the time Flora Norris stood beside him, her hands clasped behind her back, her face cut through with the wire from the dream nasturtium, her lips pressed close to imprison the hallucinatory kiss of thirty years ago.

—Tell him, Daphne, she said, unclasping her ringless antiseptic hands and uniting them in front, beneath her breast.

—Don't be afraid. Talk to him.

Daphne sat in the corner upon her straw mattress, her legs covered with a piece of torn blanket, her nightie, striped and oblong on her like a faded peppermint stick.

—Tell him, Daphne, urged Flora Norris again.

Daphne said nothing. Inside herself she thought,

They are mad. They are frauds. They are thieves who sneak through the night and day of their lives, exchanging their counterfeit whys and hows and wheres, like fake diamonds and gold, to zip them inside their leather human brain till the next raid and violence of exchanging, when they jingle their clay and glass baubles, untouched by sun, in their hands, and cry out,

—Who'll buy our answers, genuine treasure, who'll buy?

They are frauds, for the real how and where and who and why are in the circle of toi-toi, with the beautiful ledger writing and the book thrown away that told of Tom Thumb sitting in the horse's ear; and the sun shining through the sacrificial fire, to make real diamonds and gold. And we sat, didn't we, Toby, Chicks and Francie, as the world sits in the morning, unafraid, touching how and why and where, the wonder currency that I take with me, slipped in the lining of my heart, to hide it because I know. And Toby carries it backward and forward across continents and seas and does not understand it though it glitters and strikes part of the fire in him; and Chicks is afraid, and covers it with a washing-machine and refrigerator, and a space-heater behind glass.

Everything behind glass is valuable.

So Daphne thought and did not speak, and the chief of the white tribe, who wore spectacles, and carried in his pocket the sprout of a rubber tree to listen at the underground door of the heart and its beating of secret, walked forward and smiled encouragingly, saying

—Now now, Daphne, speak to me, like a good girl. We are going to make you better after all this time. You'll be home soon.

And still Daphne did not speak, so the chief tried a different subject, forgetting how and why and where, but a question, all the same.

—How are your bowels, he said. And your water?

Flora Norris moved impatiently and pulled hold of Daphne's shoulders,

—Can't you understand? she said. You're being spoken to.

And then Daphne moved and slapped the face of Flora Norris, digging her hands in the barbed wire, yet feeling for one instant the velvet and warmth of the dream nasturtium; and turning to the white chief she pushed him back to the door so that, almost toppling, he cried out a protesting

—Now now, my dear.

And with a sideways glance at Flora Norris, a curious look at the new flower growing on her right cheek, he whispered, pointing to Daphne,

—She's dangerous. Give her a sedative.

Flora Norris, recovered and withered, said swiftly,

—Certainly doctor.

And both left the room, locking the door, and peeping finally with the eyes of the world, through the hole in the door, to see if any evidence of storm remained in the small mountain room.

And after they had gone Daphne crept to the door, and poking her finger through the hole, waited there, many hours it seemed, for someone to come and hang upon her finger, a gentian or snowberry or a penny orange, or one stalk of snow-grass plucked from as high as larks fly to sing.

36

In the morning at six o'clock, half-dark for autumn, the nurse gave Daphne clothes, a pair of long grey woollen socks like Christmas and the fireplace and Toby crying because he was sick and couldn't look inside to see the presents; he was in bed, kept there until the doctor came to write his code writing in the black book and order the new bottle of pills; in bed, with a clean pillowcase and the only clean sheet, otherwise the doctor would notice, and ring up the health inspector from the corner telephone box where a man in a crimson coat and felt slippers, tore the directory in half, twice, to become the champion of the world, champion at tearing things to pieces. There are so many possible champions, you would think there is room for all people to be one and wear a medal and carry a certificate, rolled up, to be unrolled and the fancy writing pointed to with pride. And when the health inspector came he˙would have the family turned out of their home to sit in the gutter, with a penny box of matches to sell in the driving snow, and no one buying them, and the whole family, mother and father and Francie and Toby and Daphne and Chicks looking up at the lights in the rich people's houses, and seeing their feasts on the table, the white tablecloth and the candles lit upon the cake.

Yes, a pair of long woollen socks; and a pair of pants. Only
—There's a pants for you, the maori nurse said. And a striped blue smock, galatea, and a grey jersey.
—Put these on, Daphne. You're to get up.
And there was a yard full of people hopping and skipping and dancing and crying and laughing fighting and screaming and dead. Daphne sat in the corner by the wall. There were nails growing, like flowers, out of the top of the wall, except they were no colour and there to hurt if you tried to climb over.

Daphne sat all morning in the corner, and spoke to no one, only stared at the people hopping and skipping and dancing and crying and laughing and screaming and fighting and dead.

There were two girls, young, but ageless now, twins, tooth-less, crawling their sixteen years back and forth across the grey crater, their sun-stained faces fixed toward nothing, unless to the time after the Bomb and the emptiness; their throats gurgling and choking with the speech of idiocy; and their big brown eyes full of gentleness. Barbara and Leila. All day performing their dress and undress, submitting their clothes and body each to the other, crooning and wailing their animal vision of domesticity and doom. And the maori nurse watching, fat and smiling, her legs wide, her large feet cramped in the once white, now yellow, shoes; the cigarettes in her pocket, and the matches and keys; or frowning and calling in the mellow voice,
—Lavatory ladies,
grabbing the necks of the grey jerseys and the people inside them, dragging them to the door, pushing them inside; then, bawling at them, mocking them, happy with them, dressing them as a child will dress a world of witless blinking dolls that are wound for nothing save crying mama mama, and wetting; and walking half a dozen steps at a time, without direction or meaning; and the maori nurse with creek-water

eyes and paddle-flat nose, thinking—I'll have a hundred babies for my granny to look after, eh, up north in the sun.

And so passed one morning and every morning and day but the people growing gentle and together, like old bulbs without promise of bloom, thrown to the rubbish heap and sinking in the filth and blindness to sprout a separate community of dark, touching tendril and root to yet invisible colour of maimed flowers, narcissus, daffodil, tulip, and crocus-leaf stained with blade of snow.

And the night. The dormitory, and the rigid, afraid and wandering people, knowing the mountain outside and the wild storms there, huddling into their bedclothes, all of them; save Florence, sitting up to comb her hair called argent, hidden all day with the red and blue handkerchief tied across it; Florence talking, like a spell, of the places up north, and of herself being an orphan alone there, working at two years of age in the city pubs, filling the beer for the wild and bearded men; two years old, catching the tram to the city, struggling through the crowd, but travelling free because she was Florence, two years old, working as barmaid in the pub. And Florence, stroking the spell from her hair waist-long and called argent, is believed and loved and none laugh at her or contradict her dream; nor the dream of any, save the ungentle and aggressive, who wear their dream closer, the gentleness inside to the heart to keep it warm but not sharing.

And the grey crater of the long-dead mad lies empty enough to be filled with many truths together.

37

The same time that Bob Withers was beating the puppet sinner to make it cry; and Peter Harlow in the early morning of Christmas was saying, Who puts the sun out? it was Christmas on the mountain where Daphne lived.

Christmas with a pine tree that died on the third day, put in the dayroom in the corner and hung with bells and stars, though only paper made to shine but *believed* stars; and a doll angel at the top, with painted blue eyes and blonde hair and a frilly silver ballet frock, as an angel wears. And strips of

paper, all colours, spread across the room, through the mountains, the Remarkables, and in and out the trunks of the poplar
trees.

And parcels coming from nowhere, with cakes like Everest,
to be stripped immediately of snow, by the dancing jubilant
people in the dayroom; and the black earth of cake rejected,
crumbled and sodden, but mined of currants and sultanas and
crystals of cherry. And bottles of fizz popping, drunk through
two straws or three, and the awful choice between raspberry
and orange, the blood and the sun. And the night of carols,
with the white tribe smiling and kindly, the chief benevolent,
not wearing white, but a striped navy suit and a green tie, as
chiefs wear, on the side of the mountain, at Christmastime.
And the day with the red and cottonwool man, the cheat,
they say in the world, a human being dressed up, an attendant
with black suit and cuffless trousers and strong hands to grasp
and wrestle with the bewildered men on the other side of the
mountain; but real here, called Santa, smiling and giving
presents, scent and powder and underwear, and for the old
ladies a plastic apron each, all the same pattern, a red bird
flying somewhere across a green sky. And the chief there with
his fellow chiefs, all benevolent, indulgent and smiling. And
Flora Norris standing between two of the chiefs and explaining
things and pointing out people and smiling when Daphne,
with one present in her hand, returns to Santa for another—
and why not. But Santa, with the fixed smile and the hot
face, tired now, speaks sharply,

—No, no. Don't be greedy.

Daphne stands wondering and ashamed, half-turning to go
back to her seat in the corner, yet not wanting to, her other
hand still held out for the present, not pants or petticoat with
blue ribbons or talcum powder or face-cloth that the others
have been given; nor the mauve and wavy-with-flowers box
of lavender soap, four cakes in stiff twist of cellophane, which
she holds in her hand, but something different, she cannot
fully tell its name or shape or size but she wants it, needs it,
and waits for Santa, the red and white God standing in the
middle of the room in front of the angel and the tree, to
understand her need. But he cranes his human neck out of
his heavy dress of blood and frowns annoyance and impatience.

—Don't be greedy.

He pauses for her name, looking towards Flora Norris who

supplies it, swiftly and neatly, punched in holes and handled like a transport ticket,

—Daphne Withers.

—Don't be greedy, Daphne. Go away.

And seeing that the red and white God is no God, nor is there any gift nor any Christmas, Daphne begins to cry, softly, and throws her opened box of soap at the cottonwool God. The lid of the box falls off, and the undone soap spills and the room breathes of Ye Olde English Lavender, and Santa sneezes at the sharp, cheap perfume, and Flora Norris, ashamed before the chiefs, signals a nurse to take Daphne away, and her lavender soap too, for locking up.

—Greed, sheer greed, Flora explains to the highest chief.

—It's people like that who spoil the whole day.

The chief nods, sniffing the dying smell of lavender, and another smell that no one has noticed before, and that causes Flora to whisper urgently to one of the nurses who removes one patient and another and another, all clutching their face-cloths and aprons and powder (lilac and rose), quickly, to the bathroom. And Christmas is over, or never was, and the angel on the highest twig of the dead tree becomes a film-star doll from Woolworths. And the three wise men, said to have followed the wrong star, sit on the other side of the mountain, in little rooms with high-up windows and bolted doors; where they doze, dreaming the end of the journey, or wake, cursing and crying man's ignorance of the human compass and where the hand of the star points him to follow.

38

Soon after Christmas it was picnic time, with Christmas just buried, the grave filled in, and no one out walking in the sun or dark to discover the stone had rolled away.

The picnic was to be Sunday.

—Provided the weather keeps up, said Flora Norris, consulting the ward sister in the small tight room that was Flora's office, and part of her flat. She lived at the hospital, like a patient. There was nowhere else for her to live, and except that she had patients to make her bed and sweep her room and tidy her duchesse and bring her meals and papers; and polish for her; and arrange the flowers picked from the front garden; except for that, she could have been in prison herself, and was, really, in a kind of attendant and infuriating captivity, so that when her month holiday was due, every year, she felt afraid of where to go, because there was nowhere away from her prison. And sometimes she wondered—What of when I retire? What of then? I have enough money, certainly, but no place. Or what if I go mad? They have been known to, but they take them away up north, but what if it happens to me?

And then, to quieten her fears and reassure herself, she would take a walk through the hospital, with nurses holding doors open for her, and standing to attention, and the afraid, bewildered young doctors asking her advice, and the cook in the main kitchen promising to make her some cream cakes filled with cream from the farm, for afternoon tea. She would visit each ward, and if it were mealtime she would carve the roast mutton, Wednesday, or help distribute the Belgian sausage, Sunday, or watch while the Tuesday or Friday saveloys were forked on to the plates. And except that she was not borne in a chariot pulled by six horses, dapple-grey, or not treading upon a velvet carpet laid out for her from ward to ward, or not bowing and smiling with a gentle lift of her hand to the waiting and respectful crowds, she could have been a queen; so she would forget her unhappiness and, remembering the kiss of thirty years ago and the wire coiled from the grave of her lover, she would smile like a melting nasturtium: then in her power undo the smile, reshape the withered flower and retwist the coil of wire set close in her skin that was fed each night with Delicia Skin Food for the over thirties—how far over Flora Norris would not have said, but she lay each night with the white oily mask of Delicia upon her face, her pillow stained and perfumed, and her eyes, oiled a half-hour with warm cottonwool; and she would stare through the window that was barred with iron, by a frightening illusion of moonlight only, toward the slate roof of the men's side of the mountain, and their vast empty dining-room with its long scrubbed and scarred tables, and the floor of linoleum, where each day a patient with gaping idiot mouth waterfalled with slobber, would guide the electric machine that polished, revolving, whining, threatening; rebellious against effacing man's day-after-day or ingrained year-after-year torture of directionless walking.

It was fine for the picnic, at first. The chosen patients, primped and sweetened, sat like dressed and dead Christmas dolls in a world window, for someone to choose and take them and turn the key to walking and talking and dancing and real. They wore lipstick put on from the make-up box that was kept in the examination room, on a shelf with bottles of urine and poison; and charts; and a pressed appendix, shrivelled, like a leaf placed between the pages of a family Bible or Thoughts for Shadowed Days. And they wore rouge and powder and facecream from the same box, because, thought Flora Norris and Sister Dulling, that sort of thing is the first step to leading a normal life; and once they learn which comes first and where, vanishing or cold cream, they move, as one of the chiefs expressed it, in a radio talk,

—along the path to sanity, toward the real values of civilisation.

So the women were primped. And dressed very fancily, for they were travelling in the bus, and behind the bus, where luggage is kept, Flora Norris and Sister Dulling stowed a ton of good things to eat, sandwiches, paste, and tomato, and meat—trembling on the edge of a sniff of being stale; and pickle; why, so many sandwiches for the twenty people travelling, not counting the bus driver, and the attendant to light the fire and be useful in case of violence, and the nurse and Sister Dulling; why, so many sandwiches that the patients could have spread them out, like white and wholemeal squashy tiles, to make a path to walk some place, if there were any place in the world to walk to.

So they sat till the bus, big-bellied and brazen, was ready for them, and they were poured in like summer breeze and everglaze liquid; and they sat looking everywhere and afraid, and smelling the oil of the engine, and watching the ventilators, and smoothing the leather of the seats, and opening and shutting and opening the windows; and bouncing; and looking out at the other people who were not going and did not understand about going for a picnic; the patients who would have their dinner in the ward, just the same, and afternoon in the yard, and then tea, same, same, and be taken to bed, undressed, their bundle of clothes tied with the arm of a grey pullover to be put outside the door. Though perhaps there was a chance, some time in the afternoon, that a nurse would throw lollies from the window into the yard, and there would be a scramble that would end in fighting and crying, for some can grab faster, like ordinary people, and some are slow.

And while they sat there looking through the windows of the bus on to the people with no picnic, Ngaire, dressed in blue with her hair tied with a blue bow, looking very fashionable, screamed suddenly at the people having no picnic, and screamed again and again, and banged upon the window of the bus, for she was afraid, and everything was strange, being dressed in a blue dress with a blue ribbon in her hair; and the attendant hurried purposefully along to her, and they took her out of the bus, quickly, back to the day room, where she looked out of the window, longingly, like one of the people left behind; but peaceful now with nothing unknown, no strange place to travel to and eat in under strange trees and a naked sky beside a phantom and forever flowing creek of ice.

Flora Norris, watching, and waiting to say Goodbye to the picnic party, said,

—Bother. That means an empty seat. Who will go in Ngaire's place? Who is well enough to go?

And Sister Dulling, dressed in navy with white spots and carrying a straw sunhat and wearing sandals, looking very summery indeed, also said,

—Bother. There's no one.

—Daphne? suggested Flora.

—Well, if you like, but, said Sister Dulling.

They fetched Daphne and dressed her and bore her from the small hut on the mountainside to the daylight and into the belly of the red and gold monster that purred as it began to move and leapt; and later, along the hills, whined and cried, on its way to a picnic. And Sister Dulling went twice up and down the bus holding out a biscuit tin filled with sweets, and saying generously,

—Take one.

Daphne took a licorice allsort, peeling the ribbed alternate night from its yellow and blue and pink day, and sucking it to nothing, while the bus moaned and sweated, and

—Picnic, picnic,

some of the patients cried out,

—Picnic. Where to?

Sister Dulling did not answer. She was not allowed to say. It was a secret, as all the picnics were a secret, in case the world found out where they were going, and followed, to stare and laugh; and perhaps even now the world was listening, so Sister Dulling did not say where.

—It's a surpise, she said.

—But *where?*

—Somewhere, just *somewhere.*

It was a place of white manuka and a river pool of brown ice and hills of green iron; with a cloud crossing the sun, to send down a silver picnic rain like a new pin to be picked up, later, in sunlight, in the tussock, or the bald feasting-place charred with old fires and strewn with yesterday's picnic paper and bottle and sardine tin; and

—Hurrah. Hurrah,

the dead people cried out, tasting the sun and the white manuka, and had there been any dark it was folded away and shaken out when the tablecloth, like a white laden sunlight, was spread upon the ground for all to feast from.

—But the tea, the tea! said the attendant who made the fire.

—We have forgotten to bring any tea.

He held the tin of boiling water, waiting.

It was true. They had forgotten the tea. But there was a farmhouse high on the hill, and, said Sister Dulling,

—Some of us can bathe in the river while nurse and a patient go to buy tea from the farm. Surely they will sell us some tea.

So Nurse took Daphne, who had been quiet, and had not hit anyone or snatched any of the food before it was time, and they said goodbye—or nurse said goodbye, holding up the empty canister and saying,

—We'll be back with it full of tea.

Sister Dulling and the attendant waved them goodbye, and looked at each other, and at the crowd of crazy people about them, and saw how they stood happy, amazed, drinking the daylight as fast as it would spill down their senseless throats; and Sister Dulling shrugged her shoulders and said,

—What wouldn't I give for a drop of civilisation in all this mad gathering. Oh for a cup of good strong tea!

The attendant looked sly, and thought of something better to drink, he had half a mind to bring a bottle when he came on the picnic, but he knew it would cost him his job if they found out; so he agreed with Sister Dulling,

—A good cup of tea would put us right, I reckon. This gang gets on your nerves. I always think something'll happen when they come out like this, all dressed up as if they were real people. They didn't used to have fancy outings like this. I'll have a smoke in the bus, away from it all.

—As long as you keep your eyes open, said Sister Dulling.

—Oh, I'll do that all right.

So he sat in the bus, and the patients looked at him in all his glory, sitting alone and travelling nowhere; while Sister Dulling and a few patients went behind separate bushes to put on the bathing suits they had brought, Sister having her own and not a ward one like the patients; hers smart and two-piece, not down-to-the-knees and full of moth-holes.

Gasping and trembling they tiptoed into the water, their arms held across their breasts, crosswise, as the dead lie when lilies are put in their hand.

—Oh, it's cold, it's cold, they called out.

It was brown ice they waded in, splashing in sudden adventure, and then under to the neck, crouched down with their feet rubbing the green slimy stones and their hair, ducked under, like weed, matted, and smelling now of old logs and sheep's feet and earth. And Sister Dulling was the goddess. If she moved, or, not being able to swim, struck her arms through the water, the patients cried out or stared,

—Look at her! Look at her!

in a glory of wondering, for she was the goddess to be bowed down before and obeyed, on land with her white uniform and pinned medal, or in water, with her body overflowing and freckled, like a mottle of white pastry, plopping and swamping in a giant chalice of brown ice and wine.

High up, on the road leading to the farm, Daphne and the nurse stopped to rest and look down at the picnic.

—They're swimming, nurse said. Look. And it's raining down there.

Another picnic rain was falling, softly, as a reminder of silver blurring the view and white manuka, so that far below, the people hopping up and down and dancing in the water, seemed like drops of mercury grown to shape and voice, yet darting and flashing to escape the final touch or death of being human.

The farm was around the corner, in the shelter of fir trees.

It was a small building, scarcely a farm, with a plot of land fenced with manuka stakes that fell askew at the back where a black long-faced cow, a poll, stood chewing its cud, mechanical and unminding, as if the cud were swallowed and returned, swallowed and returned by pressure of a button, like a warm round penny dropped in a telephone slot.

—You wait here, Nurse said to Daphne. I'll ask about the tea.

She knocked at the farmhouse door and waited.

They listened for footsteps or some sound of life—a coughing or talking or moving, but they heard no sound, only the desolate heave of despair that fir trees give, not in any wind or storm, but out of some death or loneliness inside themselves. The air was still, save for the soft trickle of misty rain, now falling on the hill as in the valley.

No one came to the door, so Nurse knocked again, waving Daphne to keep well in the shadow, in case whoever came saw her, and knew, for any fool could tell at the sight of those gaping eyes, nurse thought. So,

—Keep back, she warned Daphne.

And knocked again. Then, impatient, she turned the handle of the door and walked in.

—Come on, she said to Daphne. We can take some tea and leave the money behind. They'll understand.

But the room was empty of furniture, and the cupboards empty, and nothing in any of the rooms, as if no one lived there.

—What a sell, Nurse exclaimed. What a rotten sell. All this way for nothing! But what about the cow, and the hens at the back, and the garden? There must be somebody living here.

She walked again through the house, opening cupboards and wardrobes.

—Strange, she said. There is no dust, it's as if they vanished, furniture and all.

It's a crazy happening, she thought, so perhaps a crazy person can explain it.

—What do you think, Daphne?

Daphne did not answer, but thought,

If I travel a hundred miles to find treasure, I will find treasure. If I travel a hundred miles to find nothing, even if I bring money with me, to lay it down in exchange, I will find nothing.

So that time of the picnic they feasted without tea, which made the nurse and attendant and bus driver and Sister Dulling very irritable; but the patients did not care, drinking sun and brown ice, even if it did taste of sheep and old logs. And they drank manuka and tussock, until the time came when the big cloth of sunlight was shaken to be rid of all crumbs, and folded up, and packed away, and the patients, toppling full of fizz and sky, climbed into the bus that sweated and whined again, going home, leaving the picnic rain and valley and hill and the black long-faced cow, melancholy now, because no one came to milk it, standing by the manuka fence, under the fir tree that heaved not in any wind or storm but out of its own sorrow.

39

The year of Christmas and picnic was a confused and strange time, not like any other time of Christmas or picnic; first, the colour of both was a white of death, the cotton-wool of pretended birth, and the star of manuka fixed nowhere for any world to follow. And the same year, in winter-time, there was a dance, where the men from their side of the mountain were encouraged to rejoice with the women from *their* side of the mountain, while the chief and Flora Norris and Sister Dulling watched, saying,

—Dance, dance. Get up and dance. What do you think we put on a dance for if you don't dance?

So the patients danced, being told to, and the women were dressed like real ladies in the same bright picnic frocks, though this was June, with the night set on the windowpanes before sundown, and the plaster walls of the rooms lined with drops of water, or

damp,

as Flora Norris called it.

—Look, Doctor, the rooms are damp. We must have them seen to.

And the chief nodded and replied that certainly he would have it seen to, or make a note of it, or refer it to someone who would refer it to the proper quarter.

Most certainly.

Yes, it was June that they danced, when in the world, as you know who live there, young ladies are being measured and fitted for their coming-out dresses; and choosing their long gloves; and between talk of swot and the music master, preparing to attend their first real ball, and be presented to the Bishop or the Governor-General, or the local member of parliament, or whoever has what is called dignity and standing in the community. Ah, June is a romantic time, no matter how cold the park seats or the sand dunes and the lupins, or the garden, that has no summerhouse now, but a little green gnome, giving no shade or sympathy.

Now, all day the men in the mountain world prepared for the dance of the evening. Most of them had a bath, queueing outside the bathroom and being warned not to waste the water; others were bathed by force, with the attendant hopping them in and out, quickly, to put clean clothes on them and make them smell sweeter than they smell every other day, working in the garden and on the farm with the cows and pigs, or shovelling coal, or sorting the dirty laundry. When the canteen opened at one o'clock those who could free themselves from their work were there to buy hair-oil and hair-cream, or perhaps a new tie, the cheating type that you pin on and do not have to struggle with; or a new handkerchief, or a pen to put in their pocket, displaying it there, as if they worked in an office, and were not patients. So that when the time came for the dance that was held from six o'clock until ten o'clock, the band arrived from town, sleek, and in evening dress, sitting on the stage, waiting, whispering together, smiling, amused. And there were the women sitting on the long forms against one wall, and the men on the long forms against the other wall, with the powdered floor between, and the smell everywhere of perfume and talcum powder and hair-oil, while the nurses and Flora Norris and the bigger chiefs sat on red velvet chairs, watching and pointing.

When the first dance began, the nurses walked up and down the wall on the women's side, and the attendants on the men's, saying,

—Dance. Dance. Go on, get up and dance!

So they danced, being told to, like real ladies and gentlemen, except the men sweated and smelt and held too closely and the women forgot to listen to the orchestra so that people had their feet trodden on, and no one apologised but laughed instead and said,

—It serves you right.

So they danced or walked or hopped or twirled round and round in the same place, and though it was a joking time, with a fine supper afterwards, no one will deny that inside was crying and confusion. The bandsmen kept darting to the back of the stage for a drink of whisky, and returning full of laughter, to play more vigorously their tango or foxtrot, while the pianist jigged up and down at the piano, playing hot rhythm.

At ten o'clock sharp the people were stripped of their finery and thrust back into the ashes, and no woman left a pink and dainty slipper of satin or glass lying on the dance floor, for the prince to find, nor was there any prince. The room was left empty and stuffy and smelling of tobacco.

—Open a window, for goodness' sake, said Flora Norris.

No, there was no magic slipper lying anywhere on the floor. If there had been, imagine the excitement, with Flora Norris and Sister Dulling and the nurses arguing to say,

—It's mine, it's mine, it fits me well,

and not knowing that to walk in its glitter they would need to hack their heel of reason till the blood flowed and they cried out with the torture of it.

40

The day after the strange time and the sitting among the dry beans in the ashes, counting two and two make five, a nurse peeped through the door of Daphne's mountain room, and seeing Daphne safe on the straw mattress, opened the door,

—Daphne, she said.

She was the maori nurse, with a bag of toffees in her pocket. She gave Daphne a toffee.

—Here. Catch. Come with me, Daphne, the matron wants you.

She took Daphne to the office where the matron sat at her desk, busy with charts and books and half-opened parcels.

—Ah, Daphne dear.

The matron drew from the corner a screen that slipped along on wheels and had a pattern on it of roses and rose leaves, two roses to each flap of screen.

—For greater privacy, explained Flora Norris. You wait there, nurse, in case I need you.

Flora Norris seemed to want everything very private. She put out her hand and touched Daphne on the shoulder. The girl shivered and drew back nearer the door and Flora Norris advanced, grim, like a close-up, her hand extended with its fingers hung like icicles.

—Now Daphne, this all comes to us sooner or later, you know, and we have to bear it, haven't we?

Daphne did not answer. She was tearing the giant roses to shreds and casting the petals in the face of Flora Norris, each petal slicing the matron's skin so that blood flowed to make a real rose blossoming upon the screen that seemed not a screen any more, for hiding behind, though who could be looking and why, except God, who may or may not be at home. Ah, thought Daphne, what is matron going to tell me?

—Are you listening, Daphne? We all have to bear it.

Daphne looked slyly at her, and smiled, because she knew what Flora Norris was taking her behind a screen to tell her. It was death. You have to hide behind a screen to talk of death, the way you cover your face with a handkerchief, ashamed, to hide your crying. Daphne knew it was death, and her mother was dead, and she waited for the matron to tell her.

—Yes, Daphne, it comes to us all, and we must be very, very brave.

Why do I talk this way, like a parson, thought Flora Norris. I'm talking to a half-wit, a loony, though one doesn't use that term now, not officially. I don't think she can understand what I'm telling her, and it's almost morning tea time, and I'm dying on my feet for a cup of tea and a bun filled with cream. I seem to have had no sleep last night, with all that dancing to take charge of, and the fuss afterwards to get them back to their wards and undressed, and then, on my rounds, seeing the rouged and powdered women, unwashed, sitting up in bed like gargoyles, with the night running down their faces and a dream smearing their eyes. Oh hell.

—Daphne, there's a telegram to say your mother died last night. Peacefully. All is well.

The matron signalled to the nurse to be ready, in case.

Daphne smiled gently, and danced the foxtrot, or was it the destiny or maxina that Francie said you dance with your heartbeats matching? Was it the maxina or destiny? Or foxtrot? Daphne could not remember. She knew it was some kind of dance but she could not remember; so she pushed the overpowering roses and the screen out of the way so God could see, and danced her dance, to music, up and down the office and then out the door while Flora Norris called

—Nurse! Nurse! Whatever are you thinking of? Get her, get her, she's desperate.

They grabbed Daphne, as she danced the last of the foxtrot, and not even picking up her dropped satin slipper, they hurried her to the mountain room where she sat alone, in the pouring rain, with no coat on, while her mother called anxiously from the door

—Daphne! Daphne! You'll get your death of cold. Come in out of the rain.

And then her mother sang the song they all knew, Francie and Daphne and Toby and Chicks; half-wailing it so that it seemed tragic and terrible

Come in you naughty bird
the rain is pouring down
what would your mother say
if you stay there and drown?
You are a very naughty bird
you do not think of me,
I'm sure I do not care,
said the sparrow on the tree.

41

Daphne stayed many days in the mountain room while the snow fell outside in a shuffle and whisper of white, and waxeyes with tiny stalks of bones sat on top of the snow-grass and swayed backward and forward in a green and yellow cloud. And then one day somebody opened the door of the room. It was the man they called the doctor, there were a tribe of doctors, in white, whirling round and round the chief, like merry-go-rounds about a tall white pole that commanded, in the centre, and we shall go to the show, yes we shall, Francie, Toby and Chicks, after we have been to the rubbish dump; to see the fat woman with fifteen men having to carry her up and down the stage, and the midget who lives in a doll's house, cooking from a tiny electric stove and sleeping in an oak bed covered with a pink frilly eiderdown made with feathers from—from, I think, from the wild swan that flew for one year and a day across the snow to the palace. No, I am not making it up, it is real. We shall go to the show and throw marbles to knock a little man from his shelf, or a toy dog that will be wrapped in silver and blue paper and given to us by the showman who smells like mattress ticking and home-brew and the inside of gumboots.

—Ah, said the doctor, politely. May I come in?

He need not have pretended, why, there was the nurse opening the door to let him in, and no one could stop him. He walked over to Daphne. She was cosy under the blankets in the corner. The homberg was full, and was covered with a page from a magazine that Olive, the goddess, had poked through the hole in the door.

On the page it said—The Lost Plantation. Chapter five of this thrilling novelette of power and passion. Then in small print it said—The Story so far.

And told of the countess who travelled, for her health, to the tea plantation owned by her cousin in Ceylon. To find her cousin dead, and a usurper, a bronzed millionaire called Gerald Whittaker, ruthlessly commanding the plantation. That is what the magazine page said, that covered the homberg, but the doctor did not glance at it.

He smiled at Daphne,

—Well, and how is Daphne today?

Daphne did not answer. The doctor rubbed his hands.

—We're feeling a little better today, aren't we?

Then he leaned nearer, as if to tell a secret, and said,

—How would Daphne like to make something, a scarf or basket, wouldn't Daphne like to make something, and go up to the class in the park with the other people; and knit and weave and sew, and not be here alone all day with no one to talk to?

Daphne did not answer, so the doctor turned to the nurse and said,

—I think we'll try her with some handwork. It will keep

her mind occupied until we arrange everything.

But it was like the woollen mills and Daphne screamed to see the mounds of wool and the dazed people picking threads, like red and yellow worms, and sewing, and digging needles in canvas, embroidering a rose, because there seemed a rule, everywhere, that roses do not grow in gardens any more but upon tablecloths and cushions and fire screens and hearth rugs, where red and green worms of wool are needled through their petals and eat their heart out, like a cancer. So the room was filled with roses and wool and people picking, unpicking, threading, stitching, weaving. And the scissors were counted and watched, and kept on a special table, and you had to have permission to touch them and hold them and use them, with a nurse at your elbow in case you decided to snip away the acknowledged and secure treasure of the real world, in one snip, leaving all of the people, the doctors and nurses and clerks and waiters and salesmen and cabinet ministers and everybody lost and severed and clinging to an unintelligible pattern of dream. So they had to watch you. But Daphne screamed at the wool, so they sat her in a corner, in the outside quiet, while her mother gave her a buttered pikelet with raspberry jam on top, and promised another, if she sat still and behaved.

It was near dinnertime when the door of the work-room opened and a woman limped inside. She wore a white smock and held a bundle under her arm, wrapped in a white cloth. She went to the nurse and whispered something, and the nurse went to the sewing woman and whispered something to her. Everything was very secret. Then the woman with the hair coloured like old clay and the white bundle under her arm limped over to Daphne and took her hand.

—Come with me, dear.

But why?

Daphne did not want to go. She had been sitting quietly, watching and smiling and waiting for her mother to bring her another hot pikelet with black-currant jam on instead of raspberry. Then perhaps she would go with Toby to the rubbish dump where they would find treasure, and write their names on the wall of the flour mill on the way, or watch the bags of flour travelling down the chute, and wondering

What if we stood beneath it, what if?

—Come Daphne.

The limping woman took one arm, and the nurse took the other arm.

But why?

They led her to a room, shining and clean and white like a kitchen and sat her on a chair in the middle of the room, and the limping woman with the left heel thicker than the right, carved thick and black like a block of licorice, unrolled her bundle upon the table, carefully, as if it were very precious, but why? It was only a piece of cloth and a pair of scissors for cutting hair and another piece of cloth like a white tea cosy. Then the limping woman whom the nurse addressed as Mrs Flagiron, spread a plastic cape over Daphne's shoulders and began to cut her hair until the floor was covered with hair, and Mrs Flagiron seemed not to know when to stop. Once, Daphne put her hand up to feel how much was left, but Mrs Flagiron gripped her arm and thrust it under the cape.

—She guesses, Mrs Flagiron whispered to the nurse.

Daphne sat still then, waiting for the limping woman to finish. She thought, This woman is from Greece. No, she has come from the underworld. I can tell from her thick arms that she has rowed herself across many rivers of the underworld, snipping the hair from the floating bodies and collecting it in her stainless white cloth, and storing it in her home that has many many rooms, yet she is able to use only one room, and soon will have nowhere to live for every room is filled with hair. I know her. I know her.

And Daphne struggled once more, and once more Mrs Flagiron gripped her by the arm and whispered to the nurse,

—She guesses.

And when the time came for the limping woman to finish, and shake out the frilly plastic cape, and rub a sweet-smelling oil over Daphne's hair, and find a hand-mirror to give to Daphne and say, smiling and pleased,

—Well, and what do you think of that? Do you think it looks all right? You know they are wearing their hair more this way now,

or this way,

or this way,

or

—Do you think a little more off this side would help? Or perhaps a thinning? Or do you prefer it tapered or poodle or urchin?

Well, when the time came for the limping woman to give Daphne the mirror and ask her advice and recommend this or that for dry scalp or reconditioning, Mrs Flagiron did no recommending or asking of advice. She had taken off all of Daphne's hair, and to make sure, she shaved the top of Daphne's head.

And there was no mirror to look in.

—And now, said Mrs Flagiron, we'll put this cap on.

And she fixed the tea-cosy piece of cloth over Daphne's head; and found a brush and swept up the hair and gathered her bundle together, and was gone, limping on her licorice foot, and Daphne never saw her again.

That afternoon the doctor came again to see Daphne. He was very cheerful.

—Well, he said, and how's Daphne?

Daphne did not answer. Her head felt naked and damp like a white hazlenut lying in the rain and snow. She kept putting her hand to feel her scalp but the last small dark shoots of hair pricked her hand with the venom of wanting to grow and having no time. She had taken off the tea cosy and put it over her chamber, over the picture of Gerald Whittaker, the bronzed millionaire.

—Well Daphne, the doctor said. You're going to have some visitors. Your brother and father. You'll like that, won't you? And tomorrow we're going to take you for a ride in a car, to another hospital, and you're going to go to sleep, and wake up better. We're going to change you so that you'll be able to live in the world and be just like other people, and you'll like that, won't you?

He drew nearer, smiling kindly,

—And who knows, in a few years time you'll be living in a little house of your own, with your family around you? A normal life, eh Daphne?

Then smiling all the time, and patting Daphne on the shoulder the doctor went out, the nurse following, locking the door, and peeping through to make sure the patient was behaving.

Daphne sat on her mattress in the corner and listened to Mattie singing. Mattie was in bed always and crippled, with a lump on the back of her neck and her face twisted so that it did not look like a face, and she sang like marbles rolling in water, knocking and gurgling, not real singing, yet it was all her speech. Daphne listened to her, and fell asleep listening, and awoke when the door opened again and the nurse came in with a letter from Chicks.

The nurse smiled,

—What a fuss we're making of you today, she said. You'd think it was your birthday, with the doctor coming to see you, and visitors, and letters, we'll have to make you nice for visitors and put a hat or beret on your head so your father and brother cannot see and be upset.

Nurse was curious.

—Let *me* look, she said, undoing the cap the other nurse had replaced on Daphne's head. Nurse touched the scalp.

—Ugh, she said, shivering. Ugh.

—Now open your letter Daphne, or I'll read it to you if you like.

Nurse opened the letter and read,

Dear Daphne, Just a short note, you know how I am with letters. I haven't written to you since after mother died. But I am really writing now, a short note, to say how happy I am that they are going to cure you, and that soon you will be living a normal life in the outside world. Don't be afraid of the operation, will you? There is nothing to fear. Do everything the doctor says, and after you are better, and it is all over, we will be able to visit you for we are coming south to live. Now, best of luck Daphne, and remember that when you are better and changed you will be able to live the sort of life I am leading, free and happy, out in the world. Now all our love.

P.S.—Do you get anything nice to eat? I am sending you a tin of cakes, bought, not home-made. These crosses underneath the letter are really kisses, all from the children who keep asking me about Aunty Daphne, though they do not know you. Love. Chicks.

Nurse made to give the letter to Daphne who covered her head with a blanket and sat still, refusing the letter. So nurse left it on the bed, saying

—Remember, we are going to make you nice for visitors.

She went out, locking the door, while Daphne took the letter and tore it to tinier pieces than snow.

42

They sat in the train, side by side, with Toby near the window, resting his arm on the ledge and staring out at the whirl of stripped willows and dead leaves and ancient logs, trapped and bearded, rising from the dark of pool and swamp; and broken fences dragged with cattle-hair and lumps of earth and river-stained sheep's wool; and crumbling farm-houses, eyeless, with their door open upon a yellow blotched throat of corridor lined with chains of decayed rosebuds and lilies. There seemed no people in the outside world, only great fearful white and red and grey ghosts of cattle prancing upon a shrivelled earth, and harnessed and blinkered draught-horses, elephantine, waiting to plough, unguided, the furrow of nothing that the luminous filled train moved through on ribbons of iron; and the startled pallor of sheep, their panic and muffle of driven grey cloud.

No, thought Toby, there are no people left.

He looked then at his father dozing beside him, uncomfort-able, with nowhere to lean his hand, so that he woke often, dazed and anxious. He opened his eyes now and looked at Toby.

—You'll ruin your good suit, he said, leaning your arm there.

Toby brushed the soot from his sleeve.

—It's all right, he said, it'll come off.

His father moved uncomfortably.

—There ought to be somewhere for the one nearest the aisle to lean, he said. I can't settle here. You should have given me the window side.

—No, said Toby. *I* wanted the window. I got there first.

His father thought of saying, I'm older, I was born first; but he didn't bother saying it. He thought instead of where they were going and what they would say and what it would be like. Would he find the right things to say? What if he were afraid? He wore his best suit, and sports coat that had cost four pounds, and a collar and tie, and he had polished his shoes till they shone like blackberries. He held his empty cigarette holder in his hand, twirling it between his thumb and forefinger.

—I'll have a cigarette, he said. And he opened a packet and planted the white stick like a candle in the silver-rimmed holder, and lit it.

—It's not a smoking carriage, Toby reminded him.

—Well, I told you to book for one.

—I'll have to open the window, with the smoke, said Toby, and struggled unsuccessfully with the catch.

—Like all carriage windows, he said in disgust.

—The old type opened better, said his father. It's these new windows that get stuck. I remember the old type opened and you could put your head out and see something. These new ones are like everything else today, fancy to look at but no use when it comes to working them. Why, the old type——

—Look, said Toby, there's wattle, or is it wattle, beginning to flower?

Bob Withers leaned to the window.

—Missed it, he said. We can't have far to go now.

—No. I wonder what time the operation is tomorrow?

—I don't know, in the morning I should imagine, Bob answered, who really had no idea what time, but felt happier saying something definite.—Yes, it's in the morning.

—Do you really think Mum would have approved?

—Sh-sh, not so loud, said Bob, looking around secretively.

—We don't want the whole world to know where we're going and what's happening.

He took the cigarette from his mouth and held it, end up, so that the holder looked like a brown and silver twig with a white bud growing out of it, and on fire with a curl of smoke.

—You get fined if they catch you, in a non-smoker, said Toby.

—We've talked over this before. Your mother would have approved. I know your mother would have approved. The doctor said this brain operation was the only chance of making Daphne into a normal human being, a useful citizen, able to vote and take part in normal life, without getting any of these strange fancies that she has now.

It was a long speech, and it frightened Bob to hear himself say it because it seemed unreal and not himself speaking. It was what the doctor had told him, the man with the long white coat and the dark glasses, in the room where a cabinet

...od in the corner, filled with files. The doctor had found Daphne's file and run his finger up and down the pages, like a man in a bank, working out sums, though nowadays there were machines to add up accounts; and he had turned to Bob Withers and spoken sternly, almost accusingly, using long words that Bob could not understand and that frightened him. And Bob had glanced hurriedly at the paper, and signed for the operation, taking the doctor's word for it, for after all, the doctor *knew*. And going out the door Bob Withers had called him Sir, he felt so afraid of him. He was glad none of his former workmates had seen him, Bob Withers, the bouncy little chap who could hold his own at smoke concerts and whose wife slaved for him. They said she even cleaned his shoes every morning.

What a wife!

—Yes, said Bob. Your mother would have approved. Daphne will be changed, sort of. I mean——

He didn't know what he meant so he sighed and closed his eyes, pretending to sleep, but listening to the train saying a tongue twister he had learned as a boy—

A lump of red leather, a red leather lump
A lump of red leather, a red leather lump.

Then it changed to—

Three tired toads trying to trot to Tilbury Towers

but somehow the whole sentence would not fit in, so he made the train say

Tired toads, tired toads, tired toads trying to trot.

And he felt a heaviness and weariness so that he would have liked to sleep for ever and not wake up because Amy was dead and there was nothing.

The train stopped suddenly, and Toby and Bob, both dozing, opened their eyes. Toby peered through the window.

—Not yet, he said. It's only for refreshments. Do you want anything? A cup of tea?

—Could do, said Bob, not stirring. He felt cold and damp, like a toad.

So Toby went to the refreshment rooms, fighting his way through the people, and bought two cups of tea and two sugar buns. He sugared the teas, using the teaspoon chained to the counter, and returned to the carriage. He too felt sick and strange, and the tea as he drank it, tasted like water-weed and clay, as if it had been brewed in a world of no people.

Why, he thought. It doesn't taste civilised.

He looked out the window at the throng of people struggling at the counter of the refreshment room, and the triumphant line of them outside, fulfilled and rested and dreamy, leaning upon the wooden bench beside their empty cups and fizz bottles and strewn crusts of sandwiches, and he thought, in his rising fear, It isn't civilised. They are not people. There are no people. And as he watched them they seemed like the heavy cattle and the doped and scared sheep they had passed, miles away now, in the waste paddocks and swamps. The train was going, in half a minute's time, the man said through the loudspeaker, but the dazed people seemed to take no notice, they seemed too tired to move, filled with clay and water-weed and red effervescent swamp water. But the train whistle blew, and certainly there were people in the world, hurrying to the carriage doors and crying out shrilly, one to the other, in a code of goodbye.

The train moved again, and Bob put his cup and saucer on the floor.

—We could slip this in our bag and no one would notice, he said.

Toby did not answer. Then he said,

—It's the next stop.

—Why do you have to keep telling me, retorted Bob. Of course it's the next stop. I didn't say it wasn't did I?

They pulled down the small bag from the rack and sat upright. Bob put on his overcoat, the tweed one Nettie had sent when her husband died. She had written Bob a letter, saying,

—Come and help me burn everything.

And Bob had journeyed down to the city and watched Nettie, his sister, the overseer in the coat factory, burn the remains of her dead marriage.

—Why, bottles and bottles of bathsalts she put on the fire, he had said to Amy when he came back.

And Amy said,

—What could she have wanted bottles and bottles of bath salts for? And to burn them? The girls would have liked them, Daphne or Chicks. But think, bottles and bottles of bath salts. What kind, Bob?

—Oh, lavender, with flowers on the outside. And old Easter
  eggs and boxes of chocolates that had gone stale and smelt
  like straw and cardboard.
And Amy had said, wondering,
—Oh dear.
And Bob had shown her the overcoat and the patches from
the factory, and the other things Nettie had given him. And
Amy had said,
—It's your size, Bob. Wear it.
And Bob said,
—I'll be dead before I wear this fancy-looking coat.
And there he was wearing it now and not dead, he did not
think.

43

They sat afraid and silent on the edge of a long
form of leather, with no back rest, so that their backs ached; but
continued to sit upright, staring ahead at the hard fire that
burned brilliantly and coldly like a coloured glacier. No
warmth came from the fireplace, and Toby and his father
shivered, gazing past the heavy fire-guard to the flames leaping
remotely and ineffectually behind their iron cage.
Toby spoke.
—It's cold, he said.
The old woman sitting next to him on the couch answered
him.
—It's warm. There's that lovely fire, she said, pointing to
the blaze.
She had come to visit her daughter, she said, she came every
week and knew the routine and was used to the strangeness.
She had beside her a brown paper bag full of cream cakes and
a thermos flask filled with tea, made at home. She and Alfreda
were going to have a picnic.
—We have a picnic every time I come, she said to Toby.
  Alfreda is so fond of these cakes and she likes tea made
  at home, instead of the hospital tea. You can understand
  that, can't you?
She spoke the last sentence to Bob who sat holding tight to
the basket he and Toby had carried between them up the hill,

fighting like children to carry it,

—Let me, no, let me. Why do you want to hold it?

—Well, why do *you* want to hold it?

—It's something to hold.

Their basket held a bag of oranges and bananas and a cake of chocolate.

—Yes, it's cold, Toby repeated.

The woman glanced curiously at him. She was going to remind them both, him and the old man with him, who seemed to be shivering yet sat muffled in that smart-looking tweed overcoat, that there was a lovely fire in front of them, and what more could they ask for on a cold day like this with the winter still hanging on?

—The winter seems to be hanging on, she said.

Toby said in a loud voice,

—*Yes, the winter is hanging on, its teeth are indrawn like the teeth of an eel and that is why it is hanging on. Whatever it swallows will never escape from the black coil of winter.*

The woman looked uncertain, and thought, It must be in the family. Some of these visitors, I've noticed, are queerer than the patients.

Bob said suddenly,

—Don't, Toby. For God's sake keep quiet. Don't say things out loud like that! Think of your poor mother!

The other visitors in the room had stopped talking and were watching Bob and Toby. And then the nurse brought Alfreda, and Alfreda's mother moved along for her daughter to sit beside her. Alfreda was a dwarf, three feet high.

—Hello, slut, the dwarf said, in a hoarse voice, and dived for the bag of cream cakes which she swallowed, one after the other, without stopping to talk, while her mother sat watching her. When Alfreda had finished the cakes she held up the thermos flask.

—What's this?

—That's tea, her mother said. Real home-made tea. We'll have a cup, shall we?

—Go to blazes and keep your tea. What else have you brought?

—There's a new pair of pants for you, from Aunty Molly.

—Pants, pants, can't anyone think of anything else but pants? And when am I going home?

She leaned to her mother, her eyes intense, her face full of scorn. Her mother smiled,

—The doctor says quite soon, Alfreda.

—Oh, go to hell.

And Alfreda got up, went to the door and called for the nurse.

—What did you dress me up for visitors when it's only that old slut, she called. Let's out of here.

The nurse, who was never far away, took Alfreda back to her ward. Alfreda's mother picked up her bag and smiling cheerfully at Toby and Bob, she went, with the remains of her picnic, to the nurse at the door to be let out.

And Toby and his father sat waiting for the nurse to bring Daphne. Bob Withers, looking about the room at the groups of visitors and patients, each, seemingly, with its separate picnic, thought, Daphne won't be like them, anyway, she'll be different. She won't swear and go on, she'll be quite different. What shall I say to her? How did she take her mother's death, I wonder? Should I say something about that? Good Lord, no.

But what if she doesn't know me?

He leaned to Toby.

—I say, Toby.

Toby was sitting in a dream, it was a fit coming, he thought, and here of all places, but how could he stop it. He knew that he shouldn't have come, and *then the cattle in the paddocks and on the railway stations, drinking their blue-lined cups of tea; their eyes and faces, and their horns growing like ivory trees, what could he do to stop it; and then the eel that was winter swallowing up the leaves and colour, and if you put your hand or heart down the throat of winter to seize what had been taken, you would have your hand and heart torn to pieces. It was a fit coming on, Toby thought, and he hadn't had a fit for a long time, not for very long, it was a fit coming on and what about Daphne, and then there was his mother too, taking up so much space. And the things to sell, at the rubbish dump, not this rubbish dump or that rubbish dump but which one; yes, surely it was a fit coming on and who could stop it?*

—I say, Toby.

But Toby fell forward suddenly upon the floor, his body writhing in the old way, his eyes vanished inwards to nothing and his face like a heavy damson plum, and where was Amy Withers to say,

—Take your teeth out, Toby. Take your teeth out.

And lay him on the sofa and put a coat over him to keep him warm, and have a cup of tea for afterwards, and words that said,

—It will go away, Toby. It won't be for always, and you will grow out of them and be like other boys.

His father knelt down beside him, saying,

—Toby. Toby.

The bananas had fallen on the floor, with the oranges, and the cake of chocolate lay near the fire that must have been warm and they had not known it, for the chocolate twisted and writhed with a curious liquid life of its own. And the nurse from the door came quickly to Toby and took his teeth out and put them upon the mantelpiece, and taking a wooden stick wrapped in gauze, like a stick of marzipan, she thrust it inside Toby's mouth, and his mouth chewed violently upon it until the fit was over and he fell into a deep sleep, his face peaceful, still flushed, and his hands clasped around the bag, now empty, that they had carried and quarrelled over because it was something to hold on to.

The nurse was calm.

—We see these every day, she said to Bob. Are you waiting for someone?

—My daughter, Daphne Withers, said Bob.

The nurse looked surprised.

—Oh, she said. Oh, I'll find out.

She went into the office and Bob could hear her telephoning. She returned.

—Go through the door. The nurse will let you through.

—But what about Toby?

—I'm afraid he can't go, it wouldn't be advisable, it will be too late when he wakes.

—But I can't leave him here.

Bob Withers was afraid. He had heard of people disappearing inside these hospitals, and then, when they said they were visitors, no one would let them out, and no one believed them. Why, anything could happen in a hospital like this, after all, it was still the dark ages.

The nurse divined his fears. She saw many visitors panic.

—You need not worry, she said. Mr Withers will be here when you return. You have to go through there to visit Daphne because she's a special.

—A what?

—A special.

To Bob Withers a special was some line of food or clothing put cheap in the shops on a Friday, for the people to buy.

The nurse led him past rows of old women in bed, sleeping, or perhaps dead, with their mouth open and their cheeks hollow, and he thought, So this is where they put the old people.

And they came to a small room with a barred window and two chairs and a small table with a vase of violets upon it, made of crepe paper, though Bob did not notice at first and stooped to smell them, thinking, They're in flower early, they must be hothouse.

The nurse watched him.

—They're artificial, she said. Don't they look real?

She offered Bob one of the chairs and left the room. Bob sat down. He had nothing to give Daphne. He hadn't brought the bag of bananas and oranges, and the chocolate had melted. How then, would he begin his conversation? He rehearsed to himself,

—Well Daphne, so they're going to make you better tomorrow. And then it will be all over.

What would be all over? He didn't quite know. As far as he was concerned everything was over, so what did it matter, and here he was, how strange, sitting in a loony cell with Lou's overcoat on that still smelt of bath salts.

He began again

—Hello Daphne. Or should it be Daffy? And why didn't they hurry. His heart was beating too quickly, he felt, and his hands were shaking, old age coming on, and he felt tired, very tired with nowhere to go because the home was dead now and the frost had got the early plums, and he remembered that he had hidden the girdle that Amy made pikelets on, away in the shed behind the gramophone and the old kitchen table, and could not bear any more to look upon it.

44

If Sister Dulling had not worn her starched uniform and veil flowing and white, though not bridal, she would have looked like a barmaid. She was broad and coarse with her pale red hair and a welter of uncomfortable fat on her body, so that she tried not to eat between meals, but smoked then, to keep her from feeling hungry; and while the nurses picked at sweets and cakes at morning and afternoon tea, Sister Dulling said,

—No thank you, I prefer·not to.

Except for an occasional biscuit when the doctor came in for a cup of tea, and

—Is your tea right? Would you like more sugar? A little weaker, perhaps? she would say to the doctor, who sat on the best chair in the office and drank from the best cup, with red string tied around its handle, so as to distinguish from the patients' cups.

And while the doctor drank his tea and smiled his glory around the staff-room, Sister Dulling would find big words to use, difficult words from the Medical Dictionary or the Shorter Oxford Dictionary that she kept in the desk for reference in writing her daily reports and sounding impressive. Other times she used the words more suited to her as a barmaid in disguise, yet a nurse too, who could talk to and tame the wild people so that they followed and obeyed her and gave her presents—the stalk of a flower, an empty envelope, a shoe-lace, a picture torn from one of the magazines, of real people living in a real house where the doors and windows open, and you know where the key is, hanging on the nail in the scullery.

The afternoon that Bob and Toby Withers came to visit Daphne, Sister Dulling herself had dressed her patient, giving her a ward skirt and pullover, new stockings, her Christmas pants, kept ready and marked with white tape, and a hat with a wide brim, the only hat she could find in the clothes room, to cover Daphne's head in case her relatives felt afraid and startled at the baldness.

—A nice hat for you, Daphne. Makes you look like a film star.

Daphne in the dead room looked up at the nice hat, seeing only its brown verandah and straw-lined eaves and feeling the heaviness of snow that had fallen all night for years upon the brown roof. She felt safe under the hat. The rain could not fall and her mother would not have to be standing at the door and crying out,

—Come in you naughty bird, out of the rain.

Daphne smiled then, remembering she was a don't care sparrow, and threw the hat into the corner.

Sister Dulling clicked her tongue.

—Your father is waiting for you, she said. You wouldn't disappoint him would you? He has come in the train.

Come in the train? If you come in the train you are always disappointed because it never takes you where you would like it to go, it takes you on and on to the waste world of swamp and mai-mai, with all the people crouched inside to break the back of paradise. Trains take you to the end. My father is disappointed whether he sees me or not, because he is sitting in his hut on the swamp, with a licence to die held in his hand and his gun ready to fire at the first sign of peace. How the snow falls on my head. I think there will be a storm.

—Come Daphne.

Sister Dulling replaced the hat on Daphne's head and led her to the room where Bob Withers sat, afraid and tired, jigging his knee because it was something to do.

—I'll be in the next room, if you want me, said Sister, with her greet-the-visitor smile.

Daphne stood in one corner of the room and looked at the man sitting on the chair. His face was pale and grey as if he had walked through dust for many years so that it clung to the folds of his clothing and covered his shoes and settled in his hair to make it grey. He has been standing up in the sky, she thought. And is covered with cloud. He has been sweeping out a crumbling house of stone. He has no wife to sweep for him and wear an apron for the children to cling to and cry in when they are hurt. I wish, she thought, I wish he would find a brush and make his suit look clean. And polish his shoes. He sits there, dirty and grey and licking his lips and does not seem to speak.

Who is he? Is he waiting for me to speak?

Pressing her lips together she sat down on the floor, first removing her hat for the sake of courtesy, as she had been taught when the sun stayed early in the sky; and watched the face of the grey man. When she took off her hat and laid it down like a laced straw well to catch the storm from the cloud, she saw the man't mouth open and his face wrinkle, as if he would cry, the way her father's face had changed when he heard that Francie was burned, and came home and saw them all clinging together like the people in the story who stuck under a spell; though not dancing up and down the cobbles of a fairy street; but crying. And the grey man in the chair, at the same time that he changed his face to look like Daphne's father crying, called out,

—Don't. Oh my God, no!

and looked at where her hair had been. With his eyes popping wide and his face afraid.

Then he said,

—Daphne. Everything's going to be all right.

But Daphne knew he was talking to himself, telling himself not to worry, that everything would be all right, though it was strange how he had discovered her name, and knew her to look at, that she ought to have had hair. And she should have hair too. Oh yes Daphne thought, I should have long hair to comb like a mermaid. But I have no hair, the woman from the underworld has taken it, so I shall put my hat on to hide that I am bald, like a front lawn or a park in the city or a picnic ground.

She put her hat on, and the grey man smiled and said kindly,

—Hello Daphne. My word, it's cold out. We haven't seen the last of winter.

Daphne smiled at him, he was so strange and grey like chalk. He smiled back and smoothed his hands together.

—It won't be long now, he said, before you're home.

Daphne suddenly spoke, in a loud voice that made the nurse peep in the door,

—What's at home? Are Mum and Dad and Francie and Toby and Chicks at home?

The nurse withdrew and the grey man smoothed his hands again and licked his lips.

—Yes, he said. They're all at home.

—Say them, then. Say them.

—You mean their names?

—Say them, and tell me.

The grey man repeated the names over, Mum and Dad and Francie and Toby and Chicks.

Daphne listened and thought, He's a cheat. He says the names as if he had learned them, like mountains, Rimutaka, Tararua, Ruahine, Kaimanawa; or like the names of towns where woollen mills are built; Bradford, Leeds, Halifax, Huddersfield. He is in league with the woollen mills and the small rooms on the side of the mountain.

—I hate you, she said. Go away. The snow is too heavy in falling and it falls criss-cross, like a tapestry, so go away.

She came forward and saw that the grey man was shivering.

—Say the names, she said, as if you don't know them. Say them new and just born.

He repeated the names slowly in a tired voice—Mum, Dad, Toby, Francie, Chicks.

Then he walked towards the door. She followed him,

—What's Dad doing? she asked.

He hesitated.

—Your father's gardening, he said. The frost has got the seed potatoes.

—What's Francie doing?

—Oh, Francie. Well, Francie's away just now. At work. At Mawhinneys.

—What's she doing?

—Oh. Peeling potatoes, I think.

—And what's Toby doing?

—Selling his scraps. He's in his truck.

Bob Withers had grown more composed. He felt in a dream, as if he were playing a fantastic parlour game and must make no mistake.

—And what is Chicks doing?

—She's playing with her dolls, dressing them and wheeling them up and down.

—We never had dolls, said Daphne. We had clothes-pegs, which were better. And what's Mum doing?

—Your mother, said Bob Withers, is making pikelets.

Then he put his hands over his face and went from the room, and the nurse, curious, watched him go down the corridor and be let through the place where the old women lay. He reached the room where he had left Toby. He expected to find the room gone or changed somehow, as if he had dreamed it, and no people sitting with baskets of food, eating cream cakes and drinking thermos tea; but everything was the same except that Toby was sitting by the fire, crouched over it. He looked blue and cold like a man leaning towards a glacier. He spoke of Daphne..

—How is she, Dad? You were quick. How does she find the life here? The nurse was telling me they play tennis and have dances.

Bob picked up the empty bag.

—Where's the fruit?

—I gave it to the nurse. Some of the patients have no visitors.

—We'd better go. We're late. I heard of someone who was locked up in a place like this, through being late.

—How's Daphne?

Toby stood up to go, and shivered with the cold of the mountain wind and his father glanced apprehensively at him.

—You're all right? he said.

—Did Daphne know you and talk to you? The nurse was telling me that some of them don't even know their own mother and father.

—Oh, Bob answered quickly, Daphne's not like that. She's different. She's not like the rest of these queer people. Different altogether, and talking sensibly.

—How does she look? Does her hair still fall over her face? Bob laughed.

—Too right, and she's brushing it away. She reminded me of Chicks the way she brushes her hair out of her eyes.

—But the operation will make her even better?

—Of course.

And back in the small room, Daphne, being undressed and put early to bed ready for the next day was thinking, I think he told me a lie about my mother. I think she was washing clothes and darning socks and not making pikelets. And I think that man was my father, no matter how much he pretended to be no relation and didn't kiss me hello and bring me a bag of fruit and a cake of chocolate; he was my father and couldn't deceive me. And my mother is sitting at home now, with a handleless cup stuck in the heel of my brother's thick grey work-sock, and darning the hole, criss-cross criss-cross, the way snow falls like snipped white wool through an empty sky. And my mother is prodding the clothes that bubble in the copper, and feeding the fire underneath with sticks of apple-box and pine cones while the cat twines about her heavy varicose legs and her feet move like laden ships, burst at the side, on a forever journey across wood and concrete seas, where the only sails are sheets, pyjamas, underpants and towels, pegged up to slap the worn winter face of a snivelling sunlight.

All this, except that my mother is dead, and I die tomorrow when snow falls criss-cross criss-cross to darn the believed crevice of my world.

Epilogue
Anyone we know?

45

It was Saturday. Relaxed in a corner of their glassed-in verandah, the manager of the woollen mills and his wife were reading the morning newspaper. The manager lay upon a rubber mattress. He wore shorts. His skin looked brown and packed tight with body, like a chinese gooseberry grown arms and legs, and hairy. His wife sat in a deck chair, her hair bound with a many-coloured silk scarf that concealed and kept in place a dozen butterfly curlers, and that waved above her head in two peaks of silk like rainbow horns.

The manager covered his face with the newspaper.

—It's hot, he said, through glass. I'll lie down and get my violet rays.

His wife leaned forward,

—Give it to me, she said. I haven't read it.

And she removed the newspaper.

The manager closed his eyes.

—There's no news, he said.

But his wife exclaimed,

—Listen to this! and read,

SOCIAL SECURITY CLERK EMBEZZLES MONEY

—Anyone we know? asked the manager of the woollen mills.

—No. And his wife committed suicide, an overdose of sleeping tablets. What is the world coming to?

And their names were Albert Crudge and Fay Crudge, though the paper said other names.

And the manager's wife gasped again,

—You didn't tell me about the murder, she said. On the news page.

—Anyone we know? asked her husband, half-asleep and warm like a hothouse plant.

—No one we know. A society woman found shot in the head, and her husband arrested for murder. Whatever is the world coming to?

And their names were Teresa and Timothy Harlow, though the paper said other names.

And the manager's wife, turning the pages, said,

—Did you read this? Epileptic convicted for being a vagabond and lacking visible means of support.

—Anyone we know? asked the manager.

—No one, said his wife.

And the name was Tobias E. Withers, though the paper said another name.

—Well, said the manager, can't you read out something of local interest, I mean something more pleasant? You women, with your thirst for crime and bloodshed!

His wife studied the social page.

—This should interest you, she said. It tells of a social gathering to congratulate one of your workers on her promotion to assistant forewoman. Were you supposed to be there?

—No, the manager said. Read on. Who was it?

—Oh someone who just recently joined the mill. It seems she had been ill for a long time, some obscure illness, but recovered after an operation. Fancy being promoted so quickly to assistant forewoman! She must be enthusiastic about her job.

—I see they've given her a wristwatch with three diamonds inside.

—What's her name again? the manager asked.

And the name was Daphne Withers, though the paper said another name.

—What else is there? the manager asked.

—Oh. Nothing. You're right, there's really no news in the paper. That is unless you count things like this photograph.

—What photograph?

—The Old Men's Home, and some of the inmates. Look at this old man sitting in the sun. He isn't even bald.

—Anyone we know? asked the manager.

—Yes, you may have heard of him. It's old Bob Withers.

And Bob Withers was sitting on a wicker-chair in the sun, looking out across the harbour of Waimaru, for the Old Men's Home was built on the Cape, and all day and night the inmates moved within sound of the sea. And Bob was deaf, and he sat alone, and slobber trickled down his chin, and his voice had grown thin like a thread, and the day burned on him as hot as the stove that is ready for pikelets if there were anyone in the world to make them.

The Women's Press is a feminist publishing house. We aim to publish a wide range of lively, provocative books by women, chiefly in the areas of fiction, literary and art history, physical and mental health and politics.

To receive our complete list of titles, please send a stamped addressed envelope. We can supply books direct to readers. Orders must be pre-paid with 50p added per title for postage and packing. We do, however, prefer you to support our efforts to have our books available in all bookshops.

The Women's Press, 124 Shoreditch High Street, London E1 6JE